Table of Contents

....1
Prologue..4
Chapter 1 – Yikes!..5
Chapter 2 – Cozy Mae's...8
Chapter 3 – Instant Replay..12
Chapter 4 – On Guard...16
Chapter 5 – Rodney's Malady...20
Chapter 6 – The Screecher..24
Chapter 7 – Assistants?...28
Chapter 8 – Oh, Sparkle!..31
Chapter 9 – The Code...35
Chapter 10 – A Silent Night...39
Chapter 11 – Yummy Sourdough...43
Chapter 12 – The Screecher...47
Chapter 13 – The Dilemma..51
Chapter 14 – Baking Bread..55
Chapter 15 – The Proof..59
Chapter 16 – Fire's Out..63
Chapter 17 – Camo Crook...67
Chapter 18 – The Big Mouth...71
Chapter 19 – The Search..75
Chapter 20 – Home Again...79
Chapter 21 – Rodney?..83
Chapter 22 – Ruth Ann!...87
Chapter 23 – The Half-Story...90
Chapter 24 – The BOLO..94
Chapter 25 – The Payoff...98
Chapter 26 – The Blue Van..102
Chapter 27 – Close Your Mouth!...106
Chapter 28 – Hello Screech..110
Chapter 29 – Joany and Cozy...114

Chapter 30 – The Simple Truth 117
Chapter 31 – Mystery Solved 121

The Screeching Shadows of Hidden Valley
Sally the Loner Mysterious Misadventure – Book 17
By Alexie Linn

Published by MA Deeter Co.

ALEXIE LINN

"THIS IS A WORK OF FICTION. Any similarity to actual persons, living or dead, or actual events, is purely coincidental."

Copyright ©2024 Alexie Linn
All rights reserved
Author photo by Fred Eschbach
Cover art by Night Café Studio

THE SCREECHING SHADOWS OF HIDDEN VALLEY

For Betty, whose enthusiasm for dragons and witches knows no bounds. This one's for you...

"*Anyone who can only think of one way to spell a word obviously lacks imagination.*" Mark Twain

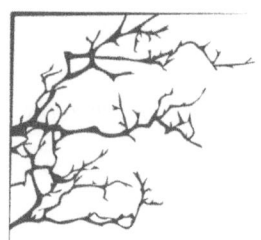

Prologue

At the end of book 16, *Too Many Bodies and a Burro*, an enigmatic wild burro had hitched a ride with Sally to Arizona.

He pulled it off by trailing down the road behind her. By the third attempt to leave without him, she threw in the towel and hauled him home to prevent his becoming so much roadkill.

And while Rodney, Sally's life-size old man doll with artificial intelligence, had mastered communicating with Cyrus (the donkey) and Tobias (the horse), the wild burro was not sharing his story. Not a word could Rodney drag out of him.

Upon arriving home, Sally named him *Bro* and laid down the laws of the land. "You're free to wander at will with these caveats:

1. Stay out of neighbor's yards and gardens so you don't go to donkey jail.
2. Do not travel on paved roads. Cars and trucks are always, always killers on the prowl.

She left his halter on him so others would know he's somebody's friend. She added a tag with his name and her phone number inscribed on it in case he had a *donkey* moment and needed her.

Currently, Bro is a free spirit. He disappears, then returns; checking in on Sally and Rodney before he vanishes again.

We join Sally and Rodney in the middle of the night a few weeks later.

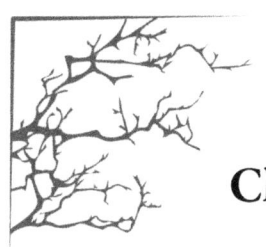

Chapter 1 – Yikes!

Sally leapt out of bed, grabbing her walking stick that leans by the doorway. "What? Who's there?" She tip-toed to peer around the curtain that served as a wall to her bedroom. Nothing appeared.

"Rodney! Did you hear a deafening, spine-chilling, growling screech?"

Rodney bleeped. "Yes, I did, milady. It came from outside. I was searching the internet to identify it. But I found nothing even close.

I thought maybe it was a jaguar or mountain lion. But no. It was not the same blood-curdling sound they make. Now I hear sirens. Had we better go look at what is going on in the neighborhood?"

Sally leaned her walking stick next to the door. "I suppose. Let me get my slippers on and grab the flashlight." Needing an impromptu weapon, she picked up the hairspray sized can of fire extinguisher and poised her finger on the button on her way out the door. Rodney followed her in his wheelchair, Amy.

"Position yourself to race back in, Rodney. I don't want you to get attacked again. Your feet can only take so much restitching."

"Yes, milady. I will aim Amy to wheel back in lickety-split."

"Thank you, Rodney. Now keep quiet so we can hear a branch crackle." She flitted her flashlight hither and yon. Nothing moved or looked out of place. No brush crunched. She sniffed.

"I smell smoke." She flipped off the flashlight and peered all around. "I see flames and flashing lights, Rodney. There's a fire in or near the community. It looks small. They should have it out fast. I think we'll be okay, but I'll get the van keys in case we have to evacuate.

Let's watch it from next to the van... just in case."

"Amy, take me to the van," Rodney ordered his wheelchair. "I will park by the shotgun door, milady so you can toss me inside fast."

Sally nodded. "Good. I'll be right out and open the door so we can swoop in if we must."

The emergency vehicles shut off their strobing lights and left the scene within the hour.

"It looks like they've got it under control, Rodney. Let's lock up and go back inside. I'm guessing I'm up for the day, but you can go back to bed if you wish. One of these days I'll catch up on my sleep... I know I will. That abrupt landing on my head from the roof has taken its toll on me."

"Amy, take me home," Rodney told his wheelchair. "I will see you inside, milady." He made a yawning sound. "I am still plumb pooped."

Sally rolled her eyes. "Yes, I can tell. And I'm in awe of all the sound effects you've mastered. I sure hope you can converse with Bro one of these days. What *is* that donkey up to...?"

With the coffee pot perking merrily and the timer set, Sally sat at the table; a notepad and pencil in front of her. She didn't have a clue why she had the notepad front and center or the pencil poised to write... but there she perched. Waiting for inspiration or instruction from somewhere. The aroma of fresh hot coffee perking saturated the air. She purred with the memories the scent brought up.

The timer beeped. She dropped the pencil; annoyed at being ready to write something but not remembering what – or what it even was related to. Hokey things like this seemed to be happening more and more often. Her 88th birthday looming large, she beat down the age ogre once again and filled her coffee mug to start again.

Re-reading Cozy Mae's letter with her coffee reminded her how fast life changes. Some changes are terrific. Others... not so much.

Sally learned of cousin Cozy Mae's existence only weeks ago. The introduction meeting was a fast and furious event that she was thrilled with. A positive change.

THE SCREECHING SHADOWS OF HIDDEN VALLEY

But the letter said Cozy Mae is now a widow. They found her husband, Clem, in his laboratory – his inventor's den – soon after Sally and Rodney returned home. A negative change.

Now Cozy Mae is trying to decide what she wants to be in her newfound freedom. Unexpected freedom that makes her feel like she's flailing at the flipping end of a whip-rope.

Where will this forced new beginning take her? Is it an unexpected gift or a downward spiral? Can it be both?

Chapter 2 – Cozy Mae's

'*He left me a legacy that you won't believe!*' Cozy Mae wrote in the letter to Sally. '*Her name is Ruth Ann. She has a sidekick. His name is Sparkle. They haven't figured out their lot in life either, except to assist me and remember him by. I'm toying with handing this 53,000-acre inheritance over to our 15-children and hitting the road. Becoming vagabonds. Vagabonds who serve a purpose. Our purpose? We don't know yet.*

You've been in our situation, cousin. What are your thoughts?'

Sally picked up the pencil again, flipping it between her fingers. "That's what's wrong! I need a bigger piece of paper to jot down all the options I can think of." She hopped up and opened the secretary she'd inherited from her mother. It was oak and very old. Older than Sally. But not older than dirt.

Her mother got it from her father, the auctioneer. It was a piece that came in to be auctioned. Grandpa was the highest bidder before anyone else had a chance.

That happened a lot when any of us – his kids and grandkids—wanted or needed what came in for auction. What were the sellers' reactions? Considering the bottles of Jack Daniels consumed on auction day between Grandpa and his cronies... they must have been fine with it. There was always a glut of happy buyers and sellers every auction day in Sally's youngster memory.

She opened the drawer and pulled out a stenographer's notebook – the kind with the spiral on the top and the line down the middle of the page. She counted the lines. "24-lines per side. I can list 48

THE SCREECHING SHADOWS OF HIDDEN VALLEY

opportunities for Cozy Mae's new life. That ought to divert her into a new-life tailspin."

Traipsing back to the table with the steno-pad Sally assured herself she's not losing her mind. "I'm just a little tired and overwhelmed by new-found cousins with new-old problems and sleep interruptions."

She included the professional mourner; bounty hunter and movie extra that Cozy Mae was already experienced at. At this time, after numb and before settling in, when her psyche is making like a whirling dervish, Cozy Mae might need reminding that all three of these previous occupations are entirely suitable for a vagabond lifestyle.

Knowing that attempting to come up with 40-plus occupations for a 57-year-old new widow with sidekicks all at one sitting would spell frustration, not productivity; Sally left the pad with a pencil on top in the middle of the table. She could let her brain shuffle in the background and jot as a single thought pops up.

By daylight, Sally had:

- Campground Host
- Writing your memoirs
- Seasonal Tour Guide
- Camp cook
- Genealogy researcher
- Gravestone Hunter

And 17 more ideas noted. With daylight comes sidetracking interruptions and chores. Chores that Sally renames '*Tasks with benefits*' when they become too many to fathom. The renaming reminds Sally that she will benefit from the effort required.

The day, like every day, zipped by like a well-siliconed zipper. Food got eaten; chores got done; rumor of a Blue-footed Booby that lives on the pacific coast and in the Galapagos getting blown off course surfaced. That sent Sally on a hunt for more information.

Rodney heard Sally muttering to herself about the Booby and stepped in to help.

"Did you say the Blue-footed Booby, milady?"

"Yes, Rodney. They say one was spotted up at the wildlife sanctuary. I want to know more. They have blue duck-like feet rather than claws. And they're big! Big like 3 feet long with a wingspan of 5-feet! That's almost taller than me!"

"Hang on, Sally. Let me do my job." He cleared his throat.

"According to Wikipedia...

> The **blue-footed booby (Sula nebouxii)** *is a marine bird native to subtropical and tropical regions of the eastern Pacific Ocean. It is one of six species of the genus Sula – known as boobies. It is easily recognizable by its distinctive bright blue feet, which is a sexually selected trait and a product of their diet. Males display their feet in an elaborate mating ritual by lifting them up and down while strutting before the female.*

Listen to this, Sally! They have parties! Can we go to a blue-footed booby party?

No. Wait. They have their parties in the water...

> *Boobies travel in parties of about 12 to areas of water with large schools of small fish. When the lead bird sees a fish shoal in the water, it signals to the rest of the group and they all dive in unison, pointing their bodies down like arrows.*
>
> *Plunge diving can be done from heights of 10–30.5 m (33–100 ft) and even up to 100 m (330 ft). These birds hit the water around 97 km/h (27 m/s) and can go to depths of 25 m (80 ft) below the water surface. Their skulls contain special air sacs that protect the brain from enormous pressure.*

THE SCREECHING SHADOWS OF HIDDEN VALLEY

Sally giggled. "No, Rodney. No blue-footed booby party for you. But I'd like to see them in action. And I hope the one visiting cousin April's sanctuary can get himself back to the coast. He – or she – won't survive here. Holy mackerel, indeed!"

Sally stopped by her growing list of Cozy Mae options. She wrote: *'Bird return to habitat service'* for blown off course blue-footed boobies.

The day ended with Sally nestling into the recliner to watch the news while she ate her supper. At sundown, she told Rodney goodnight. He responded with, "Don't let the bedbugs bite."

"Bite your tongue, old man! There will be no bedbugs in this house!"

But along about 2 AM, it happened again.

A blood curdling, spine-chilling growling screechy roar. With the smell of smoke and the sound of sirens coming soon after.

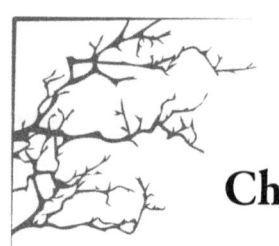

Chapter 3 – Instant Replay

It could have been an instant replay of the night before – with 24-hours lapsing for the length of the *'instant'*. The fire was in a different place and was quashed quickly.

On the third night, there was no fire to accompany the sound. Only more disruption of sleep for Sally and everybody else in the neighborhood.

Sally called cousin April. "Is there an elephant at your sanctuary? There's a nightly hullaballoo that's waking me up. It's very loud and disturbing. Sometimes accompanied by a fire.

The sound kind of resembles an elephant's rumbling trumpet. Is somebody up there having a fireside chat with an elephant?"

April chuckled. "Not that I know of Sally. But it's not impossible. You could call Christopher or Matthew and ask. It puzzles me that you would call me here... two thousand miles away to ask first."

"Well, April, me too, now that you mention it. I seem to be having more senior moments after that dive off my roof. Then I straighten up and I'm myself again. It's quite bizarre. And scary."

"That's concerning, Sally. Did you get a concussion? Could this be a residual symptom?"

Sally laughed. "How the heck do I know? I was off in some alien invasion for who knows how long... I swear it was all real and that Joany is gaslighting me. Is it a trick to get me to move to her south end?"

April laughed. "I can't imagine... but I don't know. I'll do some checking on my end concerning concussions and get back to you.

THE SCREECHING SHADOWS OF HIDDEN VALLEY

So, beyond behaving weirdly... how you been? All good with your people?" April gulped a breath before continuing.

"Drew's got a huge fireplace order in the kiln. He's trying to save them from a bad glazing compound. He's quite sleep deprived right now while he's trying to save the lot... I'm worried. But my worry doesn't stop it from happening.

I try to keep quality finger-food ready for him to grab and go with. And continue to clear these huge lawns to mow when they get dry enough between rains. The rain and wind are winning.

On the other hand, we've had no hurricanes or tornadoes to scamper from. So, I need to quit whining and go with the flow.

I read a good quote the other day. You should write it down as a reminder to yourself as well. Here it is:

'The gulf stream will flow through the straw if the straw is aligned with it and not at cross purposes with it.'

I don't know who said it. But it got my attention."

Sally purred. "I like it. I'll post it. But I'm unclear as to how to align myself with a nightly roaring pyromaniac.

I'll let you go, April. I may text Christopher. He and Matthew should show up soon to refill my sourdough pantry. Maybe they'll bring an elephant with them this time. And my hitchhiking donkey if that's where he's getting off to.

But that's another story for another day. Take care. Talk later."

Sally ended the call and stared at the unfinished list of options for Cozy Mae's future. A future with two sidekicks... Ruth Ann and Sparkle. Built by her husband, Clem. As assistants. Sally giggled, "As if she needs assistants with 15 children and umpteen grandchildren at her fingertips."

With no picture to assign to Ruth Ann and Sparkle, she was free to build her own image of the assistants. Are they metal, like the Tin Man in the Wizard of Oz? Wood like Pinocchio? Or soft and squishy fabric and stuffing like Rodney and Teague?

To be assistants, they must have brains of some sort... and mobility. Much more sophisticated than Rodney and Teague who started out as life-size man dolls. A lark for Sally and her daughter to spend quality, hilarious time together.

Lacking any defining details from Cozy Mae, Ruth Ann and Sparkle remained blank pages for Sally. Will she ever meet them? Does cousin Cozy do Facebook? Sally asked herself, "Do *I* do Facebook?"

She declared the options idea list finished. The 48 lines weren't all filled in, but there were enough suggestions to get Cozy Mae's head churning in some direction. She popped it into the mail with a hand-drawn map of how to find Sally's compound if travel was her new career choice.

Sally texted Christopher, her grandson by choice. Without Christopher, Sally may still be stuck in the Alzheimer's Care Center... lost to her people and place forever.

On the flip side of that coin, if she hadn't been accidentally shipped to the Care Center instead of to the hip repair rehab facility, she would have never met the one they call *the sourdough kid*. She smiled, finally realizing the good that came out of that horrific loading dock debacle.

It's Christopher that's game for anything. Even enlisting Sally to dance around the rules with him at a sourdough bakeoff. He's the one that installed artificial intelligence in Rodney – without her permission or knowledge. He and his friend Matthew gave Rodney his bionic arm, vision, and his wheelchair, Amy. And it's Christopher and Matthew who keep her sourdough bread box brimming with mouthwatering, tummy-loving goodies.

She shook her head out of memory lane and wrote the text to Christopher. '*Have you an elephant up there in the sanctuary?*'

He replied, '*No. We wondered if you had one down there. And if the visiting donkey with 'Bro' on his tag is yours.*'

Sally giggled. '*No elephant. No arsonist. Yes, a Bro. When are you coming to refill my breadbox?*'

THE SCREECHING SHADOWS OF HIDDEN VALLEY

Christopher's reply was a thumbs-up. To what, Sally had no clue. She let it go, assuming he's at work and busy.

An emergency alert sounded on her phone. She tapped it.

'Police are looking for an armed and dangerous robbery suspect in Stanfield. He pistol-whipped two employees to raid the cash drawer of about $20 in quarters. He escaped on foot, holding his pants up and jingling.' It went on to describe the culprit and give the phone number to call immediately if you recognize or see this masked man in a camouflage T-shirt.

Chapter 4 – On Guard

Her binoculars, mock rifle and stun-gun in hand, Sally trekked outside. She climbed on top of the water tanks and surveyed the countryside. She saw a man wearing a camouflage T-shirt making his way through the desert toward her compound.

Hopping down from the tank, she trotted into her house and tapped Detective Mulriley's phone listing. He answered on the 2nd ring.

"Yes, Sally. Where's the body now?" he chuckled.

"No joke, Michael. There's a man wearing a camo shirt slithering through the desert toward my place. He looks like the guy I just got the emergency alert for."

Detective Michael Riley gasped. "I'm on my way. Stay inside and lock your door." The call disconnected.

Sally perched on a chair where she could see out every window in her igloo; hoping any movement would catch her eye.

She held the stun-gun and air horn in her hands. With the cholla cactus consumed dry moat surrounding her property, he shouldn't be tempted to enter the compound. But to stick-up a business with only $20 in its cache sends a message that this guy isn't working with a full deck.

If he makes it through the moat and the paintball mines, Sally will deafen him with the air horn before she stuns him into a blob that she can hogtie until Mulriley arrives. Sally has put down more than one invader with her silly girl antics.

THE SCREECHING SHADOWS OF HIDDEN VALLEY

Mulriley is what Sally calls Detective Michael Riley. Before the mob invasion, his name was Richard Muldoon. While she was trying to change Muldoon's name to Riley in her head, she consistently called him Mul..riley. The mish-mashed moniker stuck. He's Mulriley to Sally. And they've been cronies for a while now. Cronies. Never friends.

Sally's proclivity for attracting misadventures – including mysterious bodies – has required the detective's presence more often than Sally would have liked. She steers clear of the powers-that-be whenever she can. It gets her dander up anytime one of them tells her she can't do that here... like live in an igloo on the desert. She goes to great lengths to stay under the radar and be the boss of her own life.

But Mulriley isn't that kind of enforcer. He's come to her rescue many times. He drops in for coffee and biscuits and chilling out under the ironwood tree at will. He told her a long time ago that she reminds him of his dear old mother. She's dead and gone. Sally isn't. But when asked if they are friends, he turns and walks away.

Sally guesses they're cronies and allows him to be on her phone list. She shares coffee with him. She feeds him. And has never regretted keeping him on her side. Ever.

He never pries into what he doesn't want to know. They both like it that way.

A screech came from points southeast. Sally jumped up and peered out the window that faced that direction. She could see a neon orange and yellow blob jumping up and down... yelling obscenities in more than one language. She watched and waited.

Eventually the blob moved toward her igloo, its fists clenched at his side. His steps are tromping and forceful. She watched. It kept coming. She saw the eyes and mouth of a neon orangey-yellow face scowling. The clothesline rope from her fanny pack lay on the recliner.

She slipped on her earmuffs to deaden the sound and stood next to the door. It came stomping into the vestibule and punched the door open.

Her finger pushed the button on the air horn. The blob screeched, covering its ears. She hit him with the stun-gun on his side. He fell like so much silly putty, sprawling and motionless.

Sally dropped the horn and gun, yanking the rope off the recliner and looping it around his feet. She pulled his feet up; jerked his arms across his back and looped the line up tight. She tied it as tight as she could and perched on the recliner arm, dreading the paintball mine clean-up to her floor once he's removed.

Noting how he was also covered in cholla cactus spines, she didn't envy the medical aid who would have to remove them – one-by-one. She smiled at the picture of this twit in constant excruciating pain while the glochids were removed – one-by-one. Then chastised herself for enjoying another's agony. But smiled like a cheshire cat again anyway.

Soon Mulriley appeared at the shredded door. "Oh! You've got him right here. All ready for me to drag out and dispose of properly." He eyed the air horn and stun-gun lying on the floor. "You really had to put your arsenal into this one. Is he dead?"

Sally shrugged. "I don't think so. But maybe. Am I under arrest?"

Mulriley chuckled. "No, but you might get sued again. Only time will tell. I wonder if he thinks the $20 was worth it."

Deputy Regent came in through the vestibule. Deputy Debbie Regent is the lead deputy. She's tall, muscular, and knows her business. Nobody messes with Deputy Regent more than once. "Here you are, boss. And is this our turkey? Is he dead? Should I call for the coroner?"

Mulriley rubbed his forehead. "Not yet. Somebody has to check him for a pulse."

"Nope." Sally shook her head. "Not dead. I saw his eyes move. He's just paralyzed from the stun-gun. But he could become unparalyzed at any moment. You might not want to dilly-dally. He'll need cholla spine removal and a bath."

THE SCREECHING SHADOWS OF HIDDEN VALLEY

Deputy Regent laughed. "You're a wonder, Ms Sally. Always amazing and good for a laugh." She clamped her mouth shut and became serious.

"But we aren't laughing about this guy, are we? He's lucky the clerks he whomped didn't die. Does he still have the cash?"

Sally spoke, "He clanked when he splatted. His pockets are bulging. I'm thinking he hasn't had a chance to spend the loot.

"Bleep!" came from Rodney's corner. "Who is here? What am I missing, Ms Sally?" Rodney rolled up next to Mulriley. "What's this orangey blob hog-tied on the floor?" He blinked his slightly off-sync heterochromia eyes. "Mulriley. How did you get here and I did not know it?"

"Hey! What about me, Rodney?" Deputy Regent pouted. "What am I, chopped liver?"

> Rodney blipped. *"**Chopped liver** is a slang expression that originated from Jewish humor. It refers to a **trivial, unimportant, or unappealing person or thing**[1]. The phrase is often used in the fuller expression "what am I, chopped liver?" to express anger, frustration, or indignation at being ignored or overlooked for someone else.* freedictionary.com.

I am so sorry, Deputy Regent. I did not mean to ignore you at all. I am so surprised to wake up and find you all here. What happened to me, Ms Sally? The last thing I remember is a horrific scream that hurt my belly. Am I dying?

---

1. *https://www.bing.com/ck/ a?!&&p=f019486c5c20bcaad15967af8abbd5df99600f3badcd4c8b2031a6c85e476c55Jmltd HM9MTcyOTAzNjgwMA&ptn=3&ver=2&hsh=4&fclid=2c897702-21f5-654e-32fd-64dd208b64b5&psq=chopped+liver+meaning&u=a1aHR0cHM6Ly9pZGlvbXMudGhlZnJlZ lZWRpY3Rpb25hcnkuY29tL2Nob3BwZWQrbGl2ZXI&ntb=1*

Chapter 5 – Rodney's Malady

Sally rolled her eyes. "No, Rodney. I'm pretty sure you're not dying. But the blast from the air horn may have tripped your overload circuit and made you faint. Or something." All eyes focused on her. "What? Doesn't that, at least, sound good?"

"I fainted?" Rodney asked, blinking his eyes fast. "I must remember to write that in my memoirs. Today I fainted from the sound of an air horn. And now my belly itches. Who wants to scratch my belly?"

Sally growled. "Oh Rodney! Nobody wants to scratch your belly! And it's socially unacceptable for you to ask them to. Sit still and listen if you want to learn what you missed."

Rodney's voice pouted. "Sitting still. Listening."

The invader is regaining strength as the zap wears off. He growls. Mulriley speaks.

"Deputy, get this guy in cuffs and out of here. I'll get Ms Forester-Newton's statement and see what I can do to jury rig her door before I return to the station."

Deputy Regent saluted the detective. "On it, boss. He'll be in the infirmary for a while getting these cholla spines plucked out. Look for us there." She removed Sally's clothesline rope from his wrists and snapped on the cuffs. He groaned.

Next came freeing of the ankles. He groaned again. She helped him up gingerly to keep her own hands out of the cactus spines. "Come on along now. The best is yet to come." She grinned at Sally and nodded as they trundled out the door.

THE SCREECHING SHADOWS OF HIDDEN VALLEY

"You got a mugga for a tired old detective who's going to attempt to make your door useable? Again! One of these times you're going to need a new door, Sally. But let me see what I can do with this one. The shadows are gettin' long..."

Sally stepped around the ucky floor to fill a mug for Mulriley. "You know where the tools are. And thank you."

While Mulriley worked on the door repair, she snagged her scrub bucket and traipsed out to the water tanks to fill it. Back inside, she added a splash of Pine sol to the water before grabbing a scatter rug to kneel on while she cleaned up the fluorescent orangey-yellow shape of the creep's body. She wadded up paper towels for a first wipe to collect any loose cholla spines before she slopped water on to scrub and rinse with.

Rodney assisted Mulriley with the door repair. "How did you learn to do that, Mulriley? I would not know where to begin."

Mulriley chuckled. "Necessity, Rodney. And logic. Experience, too. But these days you could probably find a You Tube video for instruction. It seems making videos and reels is now everyone's favorite pastime."

"So, what went on here while I was fainted dead away, Mulriley?"

"Well, old man, your Ms Sally nailed another one. This time it was one of those world's dumbest criminals.

He chose to rob a laundromat that does very little business. His total take was about $20 – all in loose quarters. And his escape plan was on foot. His third mistake was forging through a cholla infested dry moat to the property and subsequent paintball mines. His final goof-up was breaking in here. Sally was ready for him, and we were on our way."

Rodney tsked. "She is so smart. I am so glad she is my grownup. And that she did not need me to call you since I fainted and was not available to her. You missed a splinter there, Mulriley. That will hurt somebody."

Mulriley laughed. "Got it, Rodney. Thanks for your help." The detective gathered the tools and carried them out the door.

Sally swept up the sawdust and wood chips while he was gone.

"That should get you through the night, Sally. I'm sure you can handle the finishing touches tomorrow. Now I'm going to sit a minute under the ironwood tree with you unless I get a call." He picked up his mug and carried it out the door.

Sally followed, grateful for his help, but feeling ordered. She said nothing besides, "Come on, Rodney. The commander has spoken."

"This is nice. I don't get here often enough," Mulriley said.

Sally watched him from her cushioned chair, waiting to hear what he really wanted. "So, what have you heard about this recurring midnight screecher? And the arsonist that follows in his wake – sometimes."

"Ha, ha. I was going to ask you the same question, fella. It's lucky for me that his blood curdling roars come near my normal wake-up time. And I can keep a watch on the periodic fires that follow. My grab 'n' go bag, and keys are right by the door.

So, what do *you* hear, Michael? Has Sasquatch moved to southern Arizona?"

> Rodney bleeped. "*Sasquatch* – **Bigfoot**, *also commonly referred to as* **Sasquatch** *is a large, hairy mythical creature said to inhabit forests in North America, particularly in the Pacific Northwest. Bigfoot is featured in both American and Canadian folklore, and since the mid-20th century has grown into a cultural icon, permeating popular culture and becoming the subject of its own distinct subculture.*"

Sally rolled her eyes. "Thank you, Rodney... just in case we didn't already know about the creature."

THE SCREECHING SHADOWS OF HIDDEN VALLEY

"But I did not know about Sasquatch, milady – except for the time that one stole me from the van. Remember? You called it a Sasquatch. It smelled really bad. The smell made me choke."

Sally shook her head. "Oh, Rodney... you can't choke. You don't have a throat."

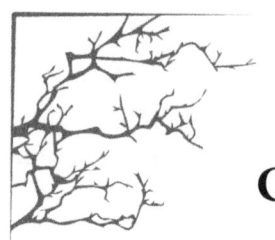

Chapter 6 – The Screecher

"I can so! Listen to this..." Rodney made gagging, coughing sounds. Sally threw her hand up. "Enough! I stand corrected, old man. You can choke. I apologize for saying you couldn't."

Mulriley jiggled to keep from bursting out laughing at Rodney's antics. He looked like he was about to choke, too.

Sally tilted her head. Her eyes narrowed. "You can hear that thing clean into Maricopa?"

He nodded. "Yes, ma'am. The deputies and I have tried to zero in on it with all the tracking gadgets we can get our hands on. It stops roaring and we have to shapeshift into firefighters before we find it. Have you heard anything from the hill about it?"

Sally shook her head. "No. And I was talking to Christopher about something... let me think... Oh! Yes! I asked him if they had any elephants up there roaming around in the night. That's kind of the noise it puts me in mind of. A trumpeting elephant.

He said no. No elephants. Or anything else that sounds like the screecher. But it's where the hitchhiking donkey has been going."

Mulriley frowned. "Hold up there. The hitchhiking donkey? We haven't visited since you left on your adventure. Tell me more."

Sally smiled. "It's nothing, really. Just a bizarre wild burro that latched onto me at my cousin's place in Texas. He decided he was coming home with me. Even to the point of following me down the road when we left. I had to go back and claim my inheritance of a donkey trailer to haul him home in."

THE SCREECHING SHADOWS OF HIDDEN VALLEY

She shrugged. "Rodney tried to talk with him. He wasn't talking. When he unloaded here at home, I told him he is free but leave the halter on for his own safety. I told him to keep out of people's lawns and gardens to stay out of donkey jail. And don't travel on roads that are meant for cars. They are killers of pedestrian donkeys."

Sally smiled. "I guess he took it to heart. I've had no calls about him. He comes for a visit and a check-in, then leaves again. I think his mission has something to do with the wildlife sanctuary. I expect we'll find out someday."

Mulriley grinned and nodded. "Have you ever just lived a humdrum life, Sally? One with no events to remember?"

Sally shook her head, smiling. "I don't remember."

The detective's phone beeped. He pulled it from its holder and studied the face. He stood, handing Sally his mug. "It's been nice visiting with you," he said and strode off, leaving Sally and Rodney wondering what now.

"First supper, then bed for me, Rodney. I'm closing the door against the night air. Are you coming in now?"

"Yes, milady."

Sally had a text message waiting when she woke up her phone. It was from Cousin Cozy Mae. It read: *'Decisions are made. I'll see you in a few days. Put the kettle on.'*

Sally sent back a thumb-up and spent the next few days wondering what the decisions were.

The driver's door opens. A tall, orange-haired plumpkin is stepping out. She's laughing. The laugh is familiar. Her matronly body jiggles. Sally's jaw drops.

Cozy Mae has landed.

"Close your mouth, cousin! Y'all are lettin' the flies in! I hope ya got the kettle on... I'm drier than a bale of straw." She patted her messy knotted hair. "I know. I clash with the van. It looks like I wrapped my head in mashed carrots. The box said brunette, not orange. Lucky for me... it should wash out in 23 more shampoos." She laughed. "Come on over here cousin. Give me a hug!"

Sally trekked over and stepped into the second squeeziest bear hug she's ever had, gasping for air to speak, "I'm so glad to see you." She stepped back to peruse the maroon van. "This is quite the outfit..."

"Yes, ma'am. My kids said to go new, never abused or stay home. They didn't want to worry about – or reconfigure – a used rig to suit me." She splayed her arms like a gameshow model. "So, I did. It has a solar panel and a built-in generator for electricity. And a portable ladder to get to the roof! I'm more impressed than anyone else could possibly be... who knew about all this stuff?"

Sally giggled. "It's for sure I didn't. I don't know what I pictured you'd be gadding about in... probably a side-by-side... but this limousine wasn't it. And I'm glad you dove into the real world.

What about these mysterious assistants? Your legacy from Clem. Where are they? They must be quieter than Rodney."

"Well, since I'm the queen bee, I shut them off if they're distracting me... like when I'm driving. This outside world can be confusing and chaotic. It's been several years since I've been anywhere with 6 lanes of cars zooming in and out like bumble bees and stoplights. The side-by-side you spoke of has been my mode of transportation for at least 10 years, or more. With 15 kidlets to do the running, I focused on the business end.

But let's wake up my assistants. You and Rodney will love them." She frowned, "Where is he? I thought he'd be at your heels."

Sally peered around, "Good question. We had an incident a few days ago. He got rattled when his body shut down. I'll go see while you wake up your helpers." Sally walked over to the ironwood tree... where

THE SCREECHING SHADOWS OF HIDDEN VALLEY

she thought she'd last seen Rodney. "Rodney? Oh, Rodney! Where are you, old man?"

She trekked into the house. He was there; plugged into his charge cord. Sound asleep.

Sally unplugged him and pushed the reset button to turn him on. He blipped and bleeped. "Thank you, Sally! I don't know what happened. I suddenly got so sleepy that I came inside. Amy plugged me in. I still couldn't stay awake. It was bizarre. But here you are. I am awake. What did I miss this time?"

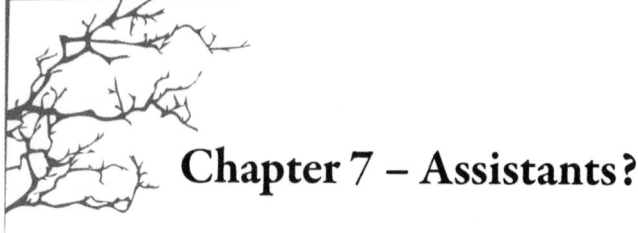

Chapter 7 – Assistants?

"Nothing yet, old man. But Cozy Mae has arrived with her two assistants. I wondered why you hadn't appeared to greet her. I left her getting her helpers out of the van. Come on now."

"Amy. Follow Sally." Rodney ordered his chair.

Sally heard them chattering before she saw them. She and Rodney rounded the igloo. Sally froze in shock.

Standing next to the open side door of the van is a young girl with long purple hair that was green when she and Rodney rounded the igloo. Now the hair is pink. And finally brown. Her skin is coppery and gleams when the light hits it.

She wore farmer john overalls over a pink and blue splatted T-shirt. Finishing the look with pink and blue hiker boots, she appeared to be mid-teen. *'Is that a tween?'* Sally wondered.

Ruth Ann's voice is sharp and articulate. "Are we there yet? I am tired of sleeping. What is this place? Do they have kids my own age? When can I explore? What if I do not like them? Can we leave?"

"Hang on, Ruth Ann..." Cozy Mae giggled. "Yes, we're there. You can explore soon. Give me time to get Sparkle out and woke up."

"Hurry, Em! I cannot wait!"

A shiny puppy stood in the doorway of the van. Cozy Mae reached under his belly. The pup sprung to life, barking. She set him on the ground next to Ruth Ann. "There you go, Sparkle. Run, snoop, leap tall creosote bushes. But don't catch a rabbit or Sally will have *you* for dinner."

"Come on Sparkle! Let us discover!" Ruth Ann waved her hand for Sparkle to follow her while she turned toward the igloo. She stopped.

"Hold on! Who are you, lady? And who is the guy in the wheelchair? He has heterochromia eyes. I always wondered what they would look like. I am Ruth Ann."

She patted the pup's head. "This is Sparkle. He is my sidekick. We are Cozy Mae's assistants. I call her Em for short. *'Her Eminence'* is way too long an expression to say all the time.

My hair is like a mood ring. It changes colors with the state of my emotions. If it ever turns flaming red, get out of the line of fire. Because my eyes are also ray guns. That is how I protect *Her Eminence*."

She stopped babbling long enough to eye Sally. "What is your name, lady? Where are we? Do you have anybody here that is my age?"

Sally gaped at Ruth Ann. Then at Cozy Mae, who stood behind the girl, grinning.

"My name is Sally. You are at my estate in Pinal County, Arizona. We live in the Sonoran Desert.

The old guy in the chair is Rodney. He is a mankin. He is my companion and assistant. While he looks like an old man, he tends to behave as an adolescent at times. About your age.

He will tell you all about life as a mankin if you let him. Rodney can also show you around the place and tell you of the booby traps throughout the property as well as why they are there.

Would you like him to be your guide and friend?"

"Yes, yes. I would. I want to explore and discover. That is what I do best. So does Sparkle. Sparkle is a cracker-jack interpreter. He can talk to anything or anybody. He then can tell me what was said. But here is a heads-up.

His flashing blue eyes are also ray guns. If his tail stops wagging, watch out and get his attention fast. Sometimes he misunderstands and makes instant crispy critters out of inert objects."

Ruth Ann eyed Rodney. "I am ready, Rodney. Let us go!"

Rodney blinked his slightly out of sync eyes. "Yes, Ruthie. You and Sparkle go to the gate and wait for me. I will be right with you." To

Sally, he said, "She is scary, milady. She never quits talking. How can I tell her anything? You taught me not to interrupt people when they are talking."

Sally frowned. "I know. You can teach her how to slow down and let other people talk if she wants answers to her gazillion questions." She waved him off. "You can do this, Rodney. But don't leave the property and mind the paintball mines."

Rodney trundled off in Amy. Slowly.

Sally gawked at Cozy Mae. "You ready for a cuppa under the ironwood tree?"

"Yes, I am! As much as I love her, she wears me to a frazzle in about 5 minutes. I hope Rodney can slow her down to a fast idle."

Sally led the tour around to the vestibule and dooryard. "If not, perhaps Christopher and Matthew can adjust her programming. They're programming and coding gurus."

Cozy Mae followed Sally into the igloo. "Oh, this is perfect for one person. I love it. I'll have tea if you don't mind."

Sally lit the burner under the tea kettle and fished around in the cupboard for a tea bag. "Is black tea okay? That's what I can put my hands on first. Or I can look for some green tea."

"Black is fine. I guess tea instead of coffee is a leftover from the great grand's raising in England. I like them all. What became of the donkey? He's not glued to you anymore?"

Sally laughed. "Nope. We still don't know why, but he goes between Cousin April's wildlife sanctuary up the mountain and here. He's on a mission for sure. We named him 'Bro'. It fits. I imagine we'll get his agenda someday. Maybe Sparkle can get him to talk."

Cozy Mae laughed. "If the outside world heard us talk, they'd put us away for sure. Robots and talking to the animals..."

Sally giggled. "But first they have to get through the ray gun eyes. I see authority figures turned crispy critter."

"Help! S-a-l-l-y... Help!"

Chapter 8 – Oh, Sparkle!

"I know that sound, Coze! They're in trouble... Come on, cousin."
Sally and Cozy Mae trotted out the door.
"Speak, Rodney! Where are you?"
"Here, Ms Sally. In the minefield. You cannot miss us."
Sally's head dropped. "Somebody stepped on a paintball mine. It's happened before. And here it is again. Get ready for baths, Cozy."
The women strode out to the trio of neon orangey-yellow blobs. "We're coming, Rodney. Sit tight."
"Sitting tight, milady. I told them both not to do it. I told them to stay clear of the markers poking out of the ground. But Sparkle was not listening. He shot his ray gun eyes at the protrusion. It shot back before it melted into a puddle."
Ruth Ann stood with her arms held away from her sides. "It ruined my outfit! Look at my gorgeous hikers! I was just walking along with Rodney when Sparkle shot his ray gun. But the pokey-outey thing shot back.

How will I ever be seen in public again? I am supposed to be your ambassador for good works. Like having someone just like me at their side. But who would want a twin of me looking like this?"
She made crying sounds. Tears actually ran down her cheeks; making rivulets in the paint that was plastered on her face.
Sally shook herself out of staring at the awesome Ruth Ann to deal with paintball splats.
"You're going to get gunky, Cozy Mae. Accept it and dive in. I'll walk with Rodney. You get Sparkle. Ruth Ann can take herself. We have to move fast to get the paint off before it dries."

An hour later, three robots stood in the sun with their electronics turned off so they could dry. Sparkle is now a splotchy silver with orangey-yellow irregular polka-dots all over his body. But Ruth Ann came clean. There are no splats of paint on her skin to embarrass her. Although a new shirt and overalls will be on her list of wants when she sees herself.

While they dried, Sally and Cozy Mae perched under the ironwood tree to visit.

Sally laughed, "That's one way to quiet her gazillion questions. I'm sure glad Sparkle didn't take on the cholla infested dry moat. I need all those glochids and spines in place. Burnt to a crisp won't serve any purpose."

"So, Sally what's all this about? Dry moats of spiny cactus and paintball mines... what else have you got around here to spook a robotic puppy?"

Sally laughed. "There's more. I have motion-activated rattlers and scorpions... wildlife cameras and electrified gates... I forget it all until something happens – like setting off a paintball mine.

It started when I came home one fall after working all summer up north to a horrific ransacking and vandalizing mess. They stole, yanked my solar system down, lived in my igloo – leaving stacks of trash on my cupboards. They dumped out my drawers onto my bed.

It was so horrible; I wanted to leave again and never return. But I couldn't. I had nowhere to go. All my life was here – on this chunk of ground.

It took more than 4 hours to make my house livable enough for me to even go to bed.

Christopher and Matthew came, as well as a few others to help me get the place put back together... and to devise a plan to prevent that ever happening again. I wanted to stave off – terrorize if you will – but not kill.

THE SCREECHING SHADOWS OF HIDDEN VALLEY

That's why I haven't been off the place for more than a couple of hours until Rodney and I came to see you."

Cozy sipped her tea, listening. "And how did that work out for you?"

Sally shrugged and smiled. "I'm not sure. My friend, Spuds, came for a visit after we left. He hung out here until I returned. So, everything was perfectly intact when we got home. Including my water tanks filled to the brim. Bless his pea-pickin' heart.

He and all my other village of mystery solvers have been godsends. And we've solved a plethora of mysteries."

Cozy Mae drained her mug. "That's interesting... a village of mystery solvers. You see, Clem built a mystery solving program into Ruth Ann and Sparkle. He knew I loved a good mystery to unwind with.

That's one of the offerings I've decided to pursue. Solving mysteries for shut-ins, hospice residents, and nursing home tenants. I want to find missing family, friends, or items that will fulfill last wishes of people so they can pass on with a happy heart."

Sally's forehead creased. "Wow! That is one tall order, cousin. I admire your pluck. Have you completed any projects yet?"

Cozy Mae nodded, smiling. "We have. We located a brother for a woman in hospice that had been missing for 15-years. They were happy as two-peas-in-a-pod when we left them.

Another wanted to know if her daughter really committed suicide. The answer was no. She saw the murderers imprisoned before she passed away.

A shut-in wanted to know why her house made creeping, thumping sounds every night. Was it haunted?

It wasn't. A homeless fella had been living in her attic for years. She took him in as a boarder that could repair and revamp her place in exchange for room and board. No more creeping, thumping sounds.

Clem did a very fine job of building and programming my assistants. Now, if I could get Ruth Ann to slow down jabbering and listen... I'd be a happy camper. And make Sparkle stop and think before he zaps would be even better." She shrugged. "But reprogramming robots is not my forte. So, I deal with it... and shut them off when I need a break."

Sally's phone chimed that a text message has arrived. She tapped and swiped to reveal it. She smiled and replied to the message before grinning at Cozy Mae. "Great news! Christopher and Matthew will be here first thing tomorrow to refill my bread box and see to other pressing needs. Shall I add adjusting Ruth Ann and Sparkle's programming to my list?"

Cozy Mae fidgeted and bit her lip. Fear creased her forehead. She ran her fingers through her hair.

Chapter 9 – The Code

"Are y'all sure they won't kill their personalities? Can they do it so that it can be undone?"

Sally tilted her head, eyeing Cozy Mae. "You're confusing me, girl... I'm sure I heard you say you want them both to slow down and think before they act. That sounds like a personality change to me. A lobotomy is a lobotomy. Whether it is done with a scalpel or coding. As all mama's say, '*Be careful what you ask for*'.

If you'd rather not take any chances..."

Cozy Mae shook her head. "No. I want them both chilled just a bit if it can be done without completely changing their character and traits. And if it can be reversed."

Sally laughed. "I see. It's like trying on a pair of shoes... or getting a dress altered to fit the picture in your head." She shrugged. "Why not? Isn't that what artificial intelligence is all about? You give it parameters and it conforms to your specs." She nodded. "I like it. I never thought about asking the boys to change Rodney's parameters. It's the Stepford Wives in real life..."

Cozy Mae's eyes widened. Her forehead creased. "Yikes! Now you're sounding ghoulish. I think I'll take my own advice and think about it more. Maybe talk to your boys first about the ramifications."

Sally nodded. "As you wish. I think that's wise. Practice what you preach." She yawned. "And it's nearing bedtime for me. Are we supping together? I have an outdoor kitchen, but it's a dot compared to your restaurant sized cookhouse. Is your rig set for the night? There shouldn't be any locomotives thundering by you in the wee hours, either. It's pretty quiet out here normally."

Cozy Mae shook her head. "I'm good. My outfit has hydraulic levelers that I'll put down. That'll keep the wobble at bay, too." She yawned. "Now y'all have me yawning, too. I think we should call it a day. I'll take my crew over and tuck them in... so to speak. I can turn a fan on them overnight to be sure they're dry to the bone before I flip their switch on again in the morning.

Do you need help with your Rodney?"

Sally shook her head. "No. He has a manual switch on Amy so I can push him. I'll turn a fan on him as well." She yawned again and rocked out of her chair. "It's catching... yawning. Do you need help with your charges?"

Cozy Mae waved her down. "No. I'll make two trips. I need the exercise. I've been cooped up for several days." She trudged over to the robots; picked Ruth Ann up and tucked her under her flabby arm. Grabbing Sparkle by the tail, she grinned. "Nope. Looks like I can do this in one trip. See y'all in the morning. I'll bring my own mug."

Sally watched her newfound cousin traipse around the igloo to her tiny house on wheels. She flipped the lever on Amy to wheel Rodney in through the portico. Parking him in his usual charge corner, she aimed a fan at his torso and flipped it on.

She heard the hydraulic levelers stabilizing Cozy Mae's van and shook her head at the wonders of technology. Then reminded herself of the maintenance issues her exquisite van will require down the road a piece. She was glad for cousin Cozy who has a myriad of fixers on her call list.

☺

Sally felt Rodney's belly for dampness when she got her coffee going at 3 AM. He felt dry. She took a breath and pushed his power button. No smell of smoking wires came. He bleeped.

"Oh, finally!" He yawned and made stretching sounds. "I had a very long sleep, milady. Did you sleep well?"

THE SCREECHING SHADOWS OF HIDDEN VALLEY

"Yes, pretty well, Rodney. Are you feeling like your old self after your bath?"

"I think so." He burped. "But that burp was not from my sound effects app. Am I broken?" He burped again. "Oh no... I feel fine..." He burped. "Why am I burping when I do not want to?"

Sally growled. "I'm thinking Christopher needs to look at your programming. He and Matthew are coming today to fill up the sourdough bread box. I'm sure they can fix you right up."

"Good." Burp. "This is uncomfortable," burp. "I want it to stop," burp, "milady. It is as bad," burp, "as hiccups." Burp.

"Oh, my goodness, Rodney! Should I shut you down again? Maybe there's a drop of moisture in your wiring."

"But" burp, "I do not want to go back to," burp, "sleep." Burp.

"Okay, then, old man. You say the word and I'll shut you off until the boys can fix you."

"Thank," burp, "you. Amy," burp, "take us to the table." Burp. But Amy didn't move. "Amy," burp, "take me to the table." Burp.

"Sally..." burp. "Amy is broken!" Burp, "She will not obey me."

"Maybe your burping is confusing her."

"But" burp, "I cannot talk without burping." Burp, "Will you bring me to the table to," burp, "the table to have coffee with," burp, "you?"

"Okay. Hang on." Sally walked over to wheel Rodney to the table. She reached for the lever and saw it was already in manual mode. "Oops! I forgot I had to turn you to manual mode to bring you inside last night, Rodney." She flipped the switch to Auto. "Now try her."

"Amy," burp, "Take me to the table." Amy growled but didn't move. "Oh, no, Ms Sally. Amy," burp, "is broken, too."

Sally growled while she toggled Amy's switch to Manual again. "Alright, Rodney. Both you and Amy need repair. I'll wheel you over. I'm sure glad those boys are coming today."

ALEXIE LINN

The paintball mines are getting to be too much hassle. But they're so effective! And why didn't I hear the sasquatch last night? Have they caught it?

Chapter 10 – A Silent Night

"Alms?" Cozy Mae asked, waving her empty mug through the open door before she entered. "Have y'all fresh hot coffee for a cousin in need?"

Sally giggled. "I do. And you look like a worthy beggar to accommodate." Cozy Mae was wrapped in a turquoise terrycloth hoodie robe with a field of daisies appliqued here and there. She smelled of toothpaste. "Please. Come in and sit a while."

Sally filled her cup. "Do you require cream or sugar, ma'am?"

"No, thanks. Just waker-upper coffee, please. I guess I'm winding down after our long journey and yesterday's fiasco. I may go back to bed."

Sally, chuckling, "That would be your choice. Things will start moving around here in the next couple of hours. The boys usually arrive with a menagerie. Bro might even come with them.

How are your kids this morning? Rodney has developed an irrational burp."

"Is that what I'm hearing? The sound wasn't regular enough for a clock or a timer. How will he get fixed?"

Sally grinned. "Why, Christopher and Matthew, of course. They'll take a look and fix his wonky programming. Teague, Rodney's brother, had a glitch after his paintball mine experience and bath, too. They fixed him in no time.

Teague is a very proper Scotsman. He was mortified that he couldn't speak in total control. He was afraid Madeline would disown him. I find it simply amazing that these fellas get so attached to us – their companions. I think Rodney is even more connected to me than I am to him. And that's going some. I'd be lost without him."

"Thank you," burp, "Ms Sally." Burp, "And good morn," burp, 'ing Ms Cozy. Talking makes," burp, "the bur," burp, "ping worse. I am not talk," burp, "ing." Burp.

Sally nodded. "Yes, please, Rodney. It's really very disruptive... the burping. Sit tight. The boys will be here soon."

"Sit," burp, "ting tight." Burp.

Cozy Mae smiled. "I'm not powering up my crew until I know I'm ready to face the world. With company coming – especially company that can repair and reprogram – I guess I better stay up. I can sleep in tomorrow. If you don't mind us being here."

Sally slapped the air at Cozy. "Pshaw. You are family. You stay as long as you want. It's time to go if you and I start nipping at each other."

Cozy Mae smiled. "Thank you. I'm still working on one day at a time. We might have been apart more than together, but he was right across the field and ready to run with me. The vacancy is devastating." A tear rolled down her plump cheek.

Sally reached over and patted her hand. "I know. It will get easier. Day by day. If you let it."

Rodney burped loudly. "How are," burp, "my new pals?" Burp.

Cozy wiped away the tears and faced Rodney. "I don't know yet. I'll turn them on when I finish my coffee. I'm sure Ruth Ann will have a hissy fit over her overalls and shirt. The paint would not come out. And Sparkle is forever splatted with orangey-yellow splotches. He won't mind. But Ruth Ann might refuse to be seen with him. She's such a fashionista."

Cozy smiled and shook her head. "Clem's legacy. Who knew? I wonder if Dad is turning over in his grave. Mom's laughing. I hear her."

A dog barked. Sally strode to the window that looks out on the parking area. She grinned. "They're here. Charlemagne is barking at

THE SCREECHING SHADOWS OF HIDDEN VALLEY

your van door. Are you sure your guys haven't learned to reboot themselves?"

Cozy Mae towered behind Sally, peering out the window over her head. "I'm pretty sure. But they're robots. And they're smart. Ruth Ann may have downloaded an app for that when I wasn't looking. She can be a stinker at times." She snagged her coffee mug. "I better go see and get presentable to the world. I'll see you later, Sally."

"Who's here, Ms Sally?" Burp. "I know that bark. Is my Christopher," burp, "here? Take me outside, Sally." Burp.

Sally stepped away from the window. "Coming, Rodney." She opened the door and wheeled Rodney out to the end of the vestibule, locking Amy's wheels for good measure. She waited with him.

Bro was the first to arrive. He trod right up to Sally, laying his chin on her shoulder and rubbing her cheek. She wrapped her arms around him and hugged the stuffin's out of him. He walked over and bumped the water bucket with his muzzle. "Hang on, Bro. I'm coming. Rodney isn't able to do his chores right now."

"Hi Gram," Christopher yelled, sliding off from Tobias, the palomino that came with the wildlife sanctuary they caretake. "Hey, Rodney. What's new with you?"

"I fainted," burp. "And I am broken. So is Amy," burp. "Please fix us first. Sally is doing my," burp, "work."

Christopher chuckled. "I see. And hear. And I will. Did Gram get a new van?" He threw his hand up. "Never mind. Don't tell me now. First, I will fix you. Then you can tell me everything. That burping business is too distracting. Sit tight, Rodney. I'll be right with you." Christopher trekked to the water tanks to give Gram a hug.

"I'll fix Rodney's programming first, Gram. Rodney the robot fainted? How'd he pull that one off?" Christopher laughed.

"It's a long story, maboy. The bottom line is I had to fire the air horn inside the house. I think the sound blast overloaded something in him.

He recovered from the faint. The burp appeared after he and Ruth Ann and Sparkle tripped a paintball mine. When I turned him on this morning, he'd acquired that pesky burp. And Amy growls but won't move. I hope you can get her going, too. You've spoiled me, young'un.

And how are you all at the wildlife refuge?"

Christopher smiled. "We're good, except for searching for that screecher in the shadows and keeping a lookout for the firebug. It seems like anything that can make that blood curdling shriek would be huge and so easy to locate... The fires have us all on the edge of our seats."

Chapter 11 – Yummy Sourdough

"I didn't hear it last night, Christopher. Am I sleeping through it already?"

He shook his head, "We didn't hear it, either." He gazed toward Rodney. He was burping at Matthew. "We better get Rodney and Amy fixed. Matthew is looking rattled from trying to talk with him.

Is your computer up and running?"

Sally shut off the water and gave Bro a final pat. Tobias and Cyrus, the donkey Matthew rode in on, stood in line for the water bucket. "It will be. I'll get you set-up and come back to get these guys settled. Is Sassy here?" Sassy, the goat bumped Sally's butt. "Oh, there you are. You all practice patience. I'll be back." She and Christopher trekked to the house.

Christopher wheeled Rodney in while Sally booted the laptop that the boys will use to fix him. Matthew followed her in.

"Good morning, Mom. It looks like we have lots to do today."

"Yes, you do. And this isn't the half of it. But you guys get started and we'll go from there. Tell me if I can help."

Matthew grinned, flashing his brilliant pearly whites at her. He smelled of Old Spice... an aroma that instantly took her back to being a kid with Daddy headed out the door to work. Daddy wore navy blue Dickies and black non-slip, puncture proof steel-toed work shoes. They were very heavy shoes. She remembered trying to walk in them when he wasn't looking. It felt like her feet were glued to the floor. They wouldn't even slide.

Matthew interrupted her trip down memory lane. "I'm sure we'll be fine, mom. I'll get started on the breads and help Christopher along the way. Rodney's irksome burp has priority."

Sally grit her teeth. "Yes, please!" She looked around. "No experimental treats came with you this time?"

Matthew laughed. "No, mom. We've been too busy with that nightly screecher to focus on sourdough research and development. Before the shrieker and pyromaniac started we were playing around with a rolled gingerbread to make gingerbread men for the holidays. We'll get back to it when that mystery is solved. When we don't have to be ready to jump and run."

Sally shook her head. "For the holidays? Have I slept through an entire summer? Yayyy."

He chuckled. "No, mom. But we have to start now to acquire perfection and get through the big giant head bureaucracy. It takes time. Much time."

Sally frowned. "Bummer. That means blistering days are still to come. Bleh!" She walked out the door again to see to the critters who are playing volleyball with the empty bucket and want more. "So, guys, what are you up to these days?" Cyrus bumped the bucket again. "I see. More water has priority for you." She laughed.

With the water bucket filled for the last time, and stopping to broadcast a scoop of cracked corn and milo out for the birds and bunnies, Sally plunked into her cushy chair under the ironwood tree.

Ms Lizzy strolled out to perch on her favorite rock to nab breakfast. She looked like a bad hair day... the tiny lizard was shedding her first skin of the season. Sally smiled, fluffing and tucking her own hair in need of styling. She wondered if Ruth Ann was dexterous enough to cut and style hair. Or what about Cozy Mae?

Having lived on a 53,000-acre self-sufficient homestead her entire life, is she the resident hairdresser? What will her 15-children et al do without her on property?

THE SCREECHING SHADOWS OF HIDDEN VALLEY

Sally heard Ruth Ann's sharp, articulate incessant questioning babble before the group appeared.

"Em, we must ask Cousin Sally where to get my new clothes. I simply cannot be seen wearing these stained rags. And what will we do about Sparkle? He is so obviously a bot now. No self-respecting puppy would be seen with all those neon splotches." Seeing Sally, she didn't miss a beat.

"Good morning, Ms Sally. We had a very long sleep. But now we are awake and ready to explore again. Where is my new pal, Rodney? Is he still sleeping?" The menagerie at the water tank caught her eye.

"What are those? Can I play with them?"

Sassy spied the visitors. She came on the run; aimed to butt Cozy Mae. Sparkle growled and aimed his ray gun eyes at Sassy. Cozy Mae shot her hand out... "No, Sparkle. No! Sit! Stay!" Sparkle obeyed. Cozy Mae breathed relief.

"Phew! I thought we were going to have crispy goat for lunch. And yes, please! If your boys can do something with these two to slow down the incessant prattle and make Sparkle wait for a command to shoot, I will have a much more doable retirement."

She chose an ironwood stump to park on. "I see I need to get a portable chair for me." She rolled her eyes, "And a new set of clothes for Ruth Ann. Where do you do your shopping?"

Sally chuckled. "About 97% I order online." She grinned. "If they ship and deliver free the next day. The rest in Casa Grande or Maricopa.

The aftermath of the pandemic is still being felt. It frustrates me to go all the way to a store and not find what I need. And so many stores have gone to online ordering that I look there first.

I haven't been to a store in a few years now. Except a mini mart. The crowds of people that have no consideration for others are too scary for me. I'm sure a psychiatrist would affirm that I suffer from agoraphobia. But I don't know that I'm suffering. I'm good with it.

Was that any help?"

Cozy Mae tapped her temple. "That's the noggin I'm programmed for. Some technology is great. But as I understand it, that's how merchants used to do business. Not online, but y'all place your order and they bring it in for ya.

What's your first choice?"

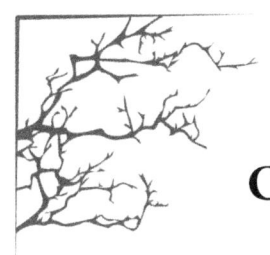

Chapter 12 – The Screecher

Chuckling, Sally said, "I start with Amazon. They know where I live. If you order through my account, there'll be no holdups for trying to find you. Walmart's good, too. And Home Depot. It all depends on what you're looking for.

Matthew came trotting out the door to the outdoor kitchen with a load of bread pans on a tray. He lit the oven; covered the pans with a clean towel; and went back inside.

Ruth Ann watched; speechless for once. For a minute. "Who is that, Em? He did not even speak to me. He did not smile at me, either. Can I ray-gun him? Can I, please?"

Cozy Mae's eyes flew wide open. Her forehead creased. "Absolutely not! Don't even consider doing such a thing! We are the visitors here, young lady. Practice proper decorum and be patient quietly.

Go talk to the horse and donkeys."

"They're stinky. I do not want to smell like them. Where is that big hairy dog I saw? The one who was barking at our door... I can investigate with him."

Sally sat up and peered around. "Her name is Charlie. And where has she got off to?

Call out to her, Ruth Ann. Just say 'Charlie! Come!' then do it again until she comes to you. I'm sure Rodney will be out soon. Then it will be your turn with Christopher and Matthew."

Matthew came out the vestibule again with a ball of dough. He shoved the bread pans in the oven; set the timer; and began rolling out the dough.

Ruth Ann called Charlie twice, but got sidetracked to snoop into what Matthew was doing. "What are you doing, man? I am Ruth Ann. Why do you not talk to me?"

Matthew gawked at the intruder. "I'm busy, mom. I'm making sourdough English Muffins. I must get them rolled out and cut so they can rise."

"Mom? I am not your mom. I told you. I am Ruth Ann. What is sourdough English Muffins?"

"They're yummy in your tummy pucks of bread."

"Em says I do not have a tummy. What will I do with my puck of bread? Sparkle does not have a tummy, either."

Matthew quit rolling dough and eyed Ruth Ann. "Ah ha! You are a bot! You have exceptional structure. Who built you?"

Ruth Ann gaped at Matthew. "I cannot tell you that. I can only tell you that I am 13 years old. Em is my main lady. I was a gift from her husband. He died. All questions concerning my structure must be directed to her."

Ruth Ann turned away from Matthew. "Charlie! Come!" she yelled. "I want to play with you." She walked away toward Sally and Cozy Mae under the ironwood tree. Sally was tossing out cracked corn and milo into the picnic ground again.

Ruth Ann questioned her. "Why are you throwing out that stuff, Sally? Is it not food?"

Sally grinned. "I am feeding the bunnies and birds. If I want them to entertain me, I must give them something in return."

Ruth Ann did a pirouette in the sand. "I can entertain you. What will you give me?"

Sally's eyes grew big. She looked at Cozy Mae for help. Cozy Mae shrugged and smiled.

THE SCREECHING SHADOWS OF HIDDEN VALLEY

"Well, Ruth Ann... what do you want?"

Ruth Ann tilted her head and put her finger on her lower lip. "Hmm. I would like a good mystery to solve. And to give someone a smile."

Sally giggled. "I believe I can reward you with that. But we won't know until the wee hours of the morning. Because, you see, the mystery does not present itself until the middle of the night."

Ruth Ann stared at Sally, listening with her eyes as well as her ears. "Tell me more."

"It all started about a week ago. We were awakened in the night by the most blood curdling screeching, roaring sounds. I thought an angry elephant was outside in my dooryard.

Soon after, a fire flamed up over in the community. The firetrucks came and stamped it out almost as fast as a rhinoceros does in Africa."

"Wait!" Ruth Ann interrupted Sally's story. "Rhinos do not stamp out fires. They run from fires just like all the animals. That is a myth that went viral from the movie, *The Gods Must Be Crazy*.'"

Sally gaped at Ruth Ann. "Well, aren't you the little balloon popper...

Do you want the story, or not?"

Ruth Ann stared back at Sally. "Of course, I do. But I must have accuracy to do my job properly."

Sally pursed her lips. "Very well. Just the facts then.

It happened again the next night. And the next night. But not last night."

Ruth Ann interrupted again. "So, it did not start a week ago. This all began four days ago. Is that correct? I want to have my facts straight."

Sally growled. "Yes, Ruth Ann. The initial blast was four nights ago. And there was not a fire every night, either. But now you've scared the details into hiding. I may or may not have told you everything."

Ruth Ann's stance didn't change. "What direction did the screeching come from?"

Sally shook her head. "I thought from the direction of the community. But it seemed to reverberate from all directions. It was impossible to tell.

The police and hunting buffs have been searching every day for the source. Are the fires connected to the shrieking?" Sally shrugged. "They don't know. It could be a pyromaniac with a gigantic bullhorn terrorizing the neighborhood. But why? To what end? Bragging rights?"

Ruth Ann tapped her temple. "Has anybody been murdered? Have there been any bodies?"

Sally shook her head. "Nope. Not a one. It is directed at everyone rather than one person or area in particular. There's been no robberies or vandalism while people are away from their homes searching for the source of the screeches or putting out fires. None of it makes even a smidgeon of sense."

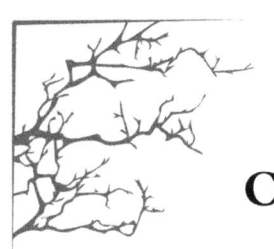

Chapter 13 – The Dilemma

Telling 13-year-old Ruth Ann the story in adult speak was right up there with expecting Charlie, the dog, to understand every word. Silly. But Ruth Ann behaved as if she was an old woman when she was gathering data to solve a mystery. Looks are so very deceiving.

Is Clem laughing from the grave at his cleverness?

Ruth Ann had one final question. "Is that everything?"

Sally nodded. "That's it. You've sucked me dry of data."

Ruth Ann nodded. "Very good. I must assimilate. I will be back." Sparkle followed her, wagging his tail continually.

Sally and Cozy Mae watched her walk away. She and Sparkle disappeared behind the igloo.

Cozy Mae shook her head, smiling. "Unbelievable. She's a piece of work, isn't she? Thirteen, going on sixty-three... older than me. Just like that. Not a drop of incessant babble if she has a mystery to solve."

Sally laughed. "You'll have to train yourself to make everything a mystery to solve. Talk about stretching brain cells..."

Rodney and Amy came flying out the door. Amy screeched to a stop at the edge of the walkway to prevent tipping over the edge. It worked. But Rodney flew out of the chair and face-planted in the sand. "S-a-l-l-y... Help!"

"I'm right here, Rodney. Do you suppose we have to start buckling you into Amy? Another add-on to your mobility pack..." She picked him up and plunked him into his wheelchair, adjusting his bionic arm onto the controls and dusting off his shoes.

"Thank you, milady. I was coming to show you I am all fixed. No more burping. And Amy is obeying, not growling. It was great until she threw me.

I must greet Matthew and the critters. I will be sure they have water in their buckets.

I do not see Ruth Ann or Sparkle. Where are my new friends, Sally? Do they not like me?"

"Pfft! Stop that, Rodney!" Sally admonished him. "It's not always about you. Ruth Ann asked where you were. And she was also looking for Charlie to explore with. But she got bored, so I gave her the mystery of the midnight screamer to solve. She and Sparkle are off solving it."

"Wait! I want to solve it, too! She is having too much fun without me. Which way did she go?"

Sally waved at Rodney to slow down. "Chill, Rodney. She's assimilating right now. You get your chores done and I'll help you look for her. Okay?"

Rodney grumbled. "Yes, milady. Rodney is chilling. Amy, take me to Tobias and Cyrus." He trundled down the walkway to the water tanks.

Cozy Mae handed Sally back her phone with the Amazon account app. "I've ordered my chair and Ruth Ann's replacement clothes. They should be here tomorrow. She's just going to have to live with Sparkle's splotches. Amazon doesn't recognize *new fur for a bot puppy*. Thanks for letting me use your account. Simplicity rules."

Christopher came out from the igloo. "Rodney's fixed, Gram. Again. Anything else before I dig in with Matthew?"

"Have you met cousin Cozy Mae?" Sally asked.

He grinned. "No, I haven't." He nodded at Cozy. "Greetings, cousin. I don't mean to be rude, but I have a lot to get to today." He splayed his hand toward Cozy Mae. "Nice to have met you."

THE SCREECHING SHADOWS OF HIDDEN VALLEY

Sally glanced at Cozy Mae. "Do you want him to work on Ruth Ann and Sparkle? I've trusted him with my life more than once. And we both lived to tell about it."

"Mmm... I don't know Sally. What if something goes awry? It would hurt my heart to damage what Clem worked so hard on to gift me with.

I think I'm going to try to tame them on my own first." She eyed Christopher. "If I can't do it, are y'all willing to try reprogramming them?"

Christopher shrugged. "Certainly. Just say the word. I can't get here every day, but I'll do the best I can." His voice warbled uncontrollably while he was morphing from boy to man.

Cozy Mae smiled. "Good. Thanks so much. I'll get back to y'all later on that." She looked at Sally's giggling face. "What?"

"Oh, nothing. It will be a fun experiment... trying to reprogram artificial intelligence like you train a child rather than coding. Let me know how that works out for you."

Cozy's face and neck flashed red. "Well, I can try. It would be just like Clem to make them trainable by me. He was a genius, you know."

Sally nodded. "Of course. I would never question that."

"Get away, Donkey!" came from behind the igloo. Sally shot up and around the house faster than a speeding bullet.

Bro was nudging Sparkle, trying to drive him the way he directs Sally toward a goal – like locating wayward mankins. "What's up?"

Ruth Ann shooed at Bro. Bro refused to be shooed. "This crazy donkey will not let Sparkle and me solve the mystery. He is trying to drive Sparkle away."

Sally used her mommy voice. "Please do not encourage Sparkle to lose his cool and attack Bro with his killer eyes. I'm sure there is a reason he's nudging Sparkle. He's a very smart burro."

"Well then, he better be smart enough to back off and leave me and Sparkle to our business."

Cozy Mae stepped in. "Ruth Ann! Simmer down. Solving this puzzle does not take priority over other's needs."

Ruth Ann pouted. "Yes, Em. He is butting in where he is not wanted. We are busy."

"Cozy," Sally tapped her cousin's forearm, "did I understand correctly that Sparkle is a polyglot? A linguist who can speak with the animals?"

"Yes, Sally. He is multi-lingual. You heard correctly."

Sally smiled. "Well then, do you suppose Bro is trying to open up to Sparkle and finally share his mission?"

"Hmm... I wonder." Cozy tucked in a wild cluster of hair that had escaped from her knot. "I say it's worth a shot to find out." She turned to Ruth Ann. "Ruth Ann, you find Rodney. He's out by the goat and equines. Let Sparkle and Bro get acquainted. Your mystery will wait. And maybe Rodney even has some input that will help you."

Ruth Ann scoffed. "As you wish, Ms Em." Ruth Ann trudged off, leaving Sparkle and Bro alone.

The last sounds Sally heard from the pup and the burro were deep-throat whispers.

Chapter 14 – Baking Bread

"Oh, Sally." Cozy Mae crooned as they settled under the ironwood tree again. "The smell of that baking bread pulls at my heartstrings. I think I should bag everything and race back to Jack County to do my part. Am I abandoning my children?"

"Wow!" Sally raised her eyebrows. "I didn't see that one coming. You could go call them and ask them if they feel deserted. Were they not pleased with your new life plans?"

Cozy tucked in the loose sprig of hair again. And again. "There were mixed feelings. The younger kidlets were the worst. They were afraid they'd never see me again. The older they are, the more encouraging they were.

They all agreed that they'd need to adjust their duties to cover my absence. But they looked at it as a mild challenge they could meet without too many bumps in the road.

Most of all, they wanted me to get off the place and reach for the stars – so to speak."

Sally inhaled deeply and exhaled slowly through pursed lips. "I get it. Grief is a process that takes time to slog through. It certainly wouldn't hurt for you to go through niece Joany's 7-day 7-step program to sort through it. I'll text her and see what she's got going. The two of you need to meet and chinwag anyway. Joan Freed is a rebel life coach and another cousin you never knew about."

Cozy Mae shoved off her stump. "I'm going to butt into the boy's business for old time's sake. Maybe that will help goose me out of this slump."

Sally texted Joany and settled back to watch her cousin busy herself in the outdoor kitchen. She tried to block the bombarding memories of being told of her own husband's death.

Blocking didn't work, but a ruckus between Ruth Ann and Rodney did.

"Did not!" Ruth Ann yelled.

"Did too!" Rodney spat back.

She rocked out of her chair and got to the bot fight at the same moment as Cozy Mae.

"Hey, hey," Cozy said. "What's going on here? Why aren't you two playing nice together?"

Tobias and Cyrus stepped back, giving the two open space. Sassy, the goat was aiming to ram Ruth Ann. Sally grabbed Sassy by the horns to stop her. "Hang on here, Sassy. Let the mama handle it."

"She called me a bad name, Ms Sally. She said I am a schmuck and that she is smarter than me. She hurt my feelings."

Ruth Ann rolled her eyes. "I did not. I was just joking, Ms Em. He cannot take a joke."

Sally raised her eyebrows. "This sounds remarkably familiar, Cozy. We went through this with Rodney and Teague on our way home from your place. It turns out that Rodney was attacked by several viruses from public Wi-Fi enroute. Ruth Ann needs to isolate herself and do a deep search and clean before she shares any more files and this situation escalates.

Rodney and Sparkle need to do the same because they've been in close contact with her."

"Oh, my goodness! I never thought of that. We've always been so protected at home. Maybe that's why her incessant prattle seemed to be even worse.

THE SCREECHING SHADOWS OF HIDDEN VALLEY

Ruth Ann, y'all heard the lady. This is not your fault. Everybody go to your corners and deep clean from the inside out. Be sure Sparkle gets sanitized as well."

"But what if Sparkle and the donkey are still in their tete-tete? They might break both my legs and make me throw-up." Ruth Ann whined.

Sally jerked to attention, eyeing Ruth Ann. "Ah ha! You've been to Rodney's Drama School. I can tell. I know about those things. I'll say to you the same thing I say to Rodney.

You have no nerve endings to feel pain with. Lose the theatrics."

Cozy Mae grinned. "Y'all heard the lady, Ruth Ann. Your Royal Eminence has spoken. Y'all must obey. Chop-chop."

Her head hung; her eyes facing the ground; Ruth Ann kicked pebbles on her way around the igloo to scan her systems for viruses, malware, trojan horses, and worms.

Sally laughed. "When Rodney had to do this—on the way home from your place—he, of course, made a big dragon slaying affair out of it. It was pretty wild. And it took a while. His brother, Teague, took care of his invasion in silence other than a grunt that escaped once in a while.

It was so good to have his own sweet self back when the whole affair was over. Rodney is normally a lover, not a fighter. Ruth Ann, as you know her, will be back when she gets through scrubbing."

Cozy let out a long exhale like she'd been holding her breath. "Lordy, I hope so. Her snarky and snarly attitude is one of the many reasons I'm considering slithering back home and returning the van. I don't know what I was thinking when I got myself into this caper."

Sally laughed. "I do. Been there and done that, cousin. Comes with grief territory. I hit the road with my friend in my old Chrysler 5th avenue. We tented for the entire summer. Rode the ferries, visited old friends, made valued new friends, roughed it and thunder egg hunted eastern Oregon.

I took her home, then I did it again. By myself. I could sleep in the car. And I did. When I settled down, I continued to work a seasonal job near Flagstaff every summer for the next 15 years. Until the marauders tore my place apart.

Another cousin traded in her sensible Nissan runabout for a baby blue Pontiac Trans Am when she became a widow. She grabbed her teenager, and they hit the road for several months. Then she settled down, turned the muscle car in for a sensible 4-door, and went to work as a church secretary to pay off her credit cards.

We do out of character things when life goes wonky on us. With any luck we land safely; none the worse for wear."

Chapter 15 – The Proof

'*What do you need, Aunty?*' read the text from Joany.

Sally laughed. '*I forgot. Cousin Cozy Mae is here. Come at your convenience to meet and greet.*'

Joany replied with a thumb-up.

Christopher and Matthew came from the igloo. "You're all filled up again, Gram. Do you need anything else before we head home on our trusty steeds?"

Sally smiled at him. "I can't think of anything at the moment. Thank you, thank you for taking such good care of me. I appreciate the both of you so very much. I'll text if Cozy Mae decides to have Ruth Ann and Sparkle reprogrammed.

Right now, they are deep cleaning their innards in search of viruses they may have picked up from public Wi-Fi. That may take care of the issues."

Christopher nodded. Matthew laughed knowingly. "Oh, mom! That public Wi-Fi can be like a bomb exploding in the coding. It is wise to clean first before fussing with their mainbrains."

Perched on Tobias, Christopher held Cyrus's reins and called out to Charlie. Charlie came from the igloo, licking her chops. "Uh-oh. What have you gotten into, Charlie?"

"I'll go see," Matthew covered the space in about three giant steps. "It's ok!" He yelled from inside, returning within a minute. "It was just a butter wrapper she licked clean." He sprawled his lanky body over Cyrus; flung one leg over the donkey's back and sat up; his toes only inches from the ground. He took the rein from Christopher.

Sassy, the goat, went on ahead, munching her way out of the compound; stopping to graze along the lane while she waited for the parade. Charlie, the dog, ran ahead; stopped to look back; then trotted back to bring up the rear until something more fun grabbed her attention – like a lizard, a rabbit, or a bird.

Christopher smiled and waved. "Until next time, Gram."

Sally and Cozy smiled and waved back.

Bro nuzzled Sally's cheek and joined the procession that was headed up the mountain to the wildlife refuge.

Eying Cozy Mae, Sally rocked herself out of her cushy chair. "I'm raiding the bread box. Will you be joining me?"

Cozy Mae laughed. "Wild horses couldn't stop me. Ah've been wiping drool for a couple of hours now."

Two sourdough English muffins oozing butter and jam later, Sally yawned. "It must be time for a nap. I'm going to stretch out here in my recliner for a bit. You've got my number if you need me.", Laying back in the chair Sally flipped on the TV and closed her eyes.

Rodney made flipping through files sounds in his charge corner while he searched for viruses.

Cozy Mae tiptoed out the door, leaving them to their break amongst chaos.

Sally jerked awake. Then she heard why she was so rudely yanked out of an excellent dream. The screecher is at it again.

Dark had arrived while she napped. She kicked the chair upright and flipped off the TV.

"Yes, milady." Rodney spoke from the window. "It is back. I am on fire watch. No flames have appeared, or sirens have sounded so far. I do not smell smoke, either."

She slid to the edge of the recliner seat. "Thank you, Rodney. It's good you're looking out for us. What time is it?"

Rodney blipped. "At the tone the time will be 1:37 AM. Beeep."

THE SCREECHING SHADOWS OF HIDDEN VALLEY

Sally rubbed her eyes. "Wow! I must have been plumb worn to a frazzle!"

Chills raced from her head to her toe when the elephant in the room let loose again. Pounding on the door jarred her from the other direction.

"Can we come in? Are y'all okay in there?" A puppy bark added to the commotion.

"Come! We're good."

The door opened. Cozy Mae, wrapped in her daisy field robe with the hood up, Ruth Ann with white hair, and Sparkle rushed in. "Is that the spine-chilling sound you spoke of?"

"It is. Rodney's on fire watch. I was still sound asleep in my chair when it let loose. I almost peed my pants."

Cozy Mae chuckled. "I get that. It's amazing nobody can find where it's coming from. Whatever's doing it has got to be huge!"

Sparkle nosed his way to the window. His ears stood straight up. When the screecher let loose again, Sparkle's ears lit up and wobbled to and fro like an antenna trying to zero in on the best signal.

Ruth Ann's hair changed colors like a strobing Christmas star light on the wall of a house.

"I see the fire, milady! We need to get ready! Amy. Take me to the van."

Sirens sounded in the distance. "Get your gear together, Cozy... we might have to evacuate in a hurry. Everybody out of the pool!"

Ruth Ann's hair turned white again. Sparkle let his ears drop and ran out the door barking. Cozy tightened her robe around her and followed her charges out. Sally grabbed the keys and her coffee mug before she trotted out the door.

At the van, she opened the passenger door and, after looking at her mug questioningly, set it on the console. The keys she gripped in her hand. "You ready to jump in and go, Cozy?"

"Yes, ma'am. I will have to follow y'all. This is all new country to me."

"Well," Sally tugged her ear, "depending on which way the wind is blowing... we'll head for Joany's first. If it's safe there, we'll stay. If not, we'll get her and Jenny into our brigade anyway.

So far, they've been able to get the fire out, but I don't want to tempt fate. I'm scared to death of fire. Someday I might figure out why.

Chapter 16 – Fire's Out

Daylight came too soon. Sally stayed up and made the coffee to splash into her mug that she'd carried to the van and back. She still wonders how the mug wound up in her hand but failed to nab her phone.

Cozy Mae went back to bed when all was said and done. "Ah've had to sleep piecemeal through fire and flood for forever, as far as I can remember. Ah'll see y'all in a few hours." She yawned. "Come on, family." Ruth Ann, her hair brown again, and Sparkle followed her into the camper.

Sally pondered the events of the night while she enjoyed her eggs and jam-slathered english muffin. She wiped the jam from the corners of her mouth and washed it all down with fresh hot coffee.

Pictures of angry elephants and fire stamping rhinos flitted through her head. Neither made any sense to explain the screeching shadows.

Is there a new scavenger hunt game out that involves blasting broadcasts for other players to locate them? Like geo-caching but with ear piercing sound rather than GPS coordinates. But what about the fires? Are they part of the game? Or is one of the players a pyromaniac just to confuse the issue? "Well...," she said to no one. "It's working. I'm thoroughly confused."

"What is that you said, milady?" Rodney asked from his charge corner. I guess one could call it his kitchen table since it's where he dines on electricity and does his best thinking.

"It was nothing, Rodney. I was just thinking out loud about the pyromaniacal elephant in the neighborhood. I was wondering if it was a new scavenger hunt game like geocaching... but the hints are the screechy roars through a megaphone. The object is to be the first to locate the screecher. And then laugh a lot, I guess." She ogled Rodney across the room. "Are the fires the signal to the others in the game that they found the screecher?"

Rodney bleeped. "I can do a deep search on the dark web, Sally. Will that help? You might have nailed it."

Sally chuckled. "If you wish. I would not deny you such a journey. But be careful. Don't get sucked into something dastardly."

"I will be careful, milady. I will route my footprint through several countries so they cannot locate me. At least I have heard that is the proper way to stay incognito. Here I go..." Rodney blipped and bleeped then settled into a quiet ticking sound. Like a metronome. First, she likened the sound to a clock ticking. But then realized it fluctuated in beats per minute... like someone is messing with the timing.

Sally cleared the table and asked, "What's next?"

She forgot that asking *'what's next?'* is like praying for patience... something will happen that will force you to grow patience. *'What's next?'* opens the door to whatever's out there.

The ruckus outside began as a simple rattling of pots and pans. But it grew fast and furious to a crash, bang, kerplunk. The kerplunk at the end was more disconcerting than the crash banging.

Sally stepped to the end of the vestibule and peered toward the water tanks. Nothing out of the ordinary was visible. Except two boots sticking toes up...like they had feet in them...from the outdoor kitchen aisleway.

She stepped back into the igloo. "Rodney."

Only the metronome ticking came back at her. "Rodney!" she said louder.

The metronome ticked faster.

She locked the door, snagged her walking stick and trekked across the room to Rodney's kitchen. She poked the mankin here and there with her stick, one eye keeping a watch on the door. "Rodney! Wake up!" She poked him again all over his body.

"I am back! Stop poking me with that stick! I heard you the first time, milady, but could not get back to you. I was stuck in a deep crevasse in the dark web."

Pounding on the door frightened Sally. "Sally! Let me in unless y'all want me to break a window!" It was Cozy Mae's voice at the door.

"Oh!" She trotted to the door; unlocked it and opened it to Cozy Mae and her bots. "Sorry. I didn't know it was you. I guess you would have heard it, too.

I came in to get my stick and alert Rodney to the boots facing toes-up in the outdoor kitchen before I went to investigate further." She frowned. "He was stuck in the dark web. And all I did was ask 'what's next?' while I looked for my list when all you-know-what broke loose."

"What else y'all got besides the stick?" Cozy asked.

Sally pointed toward the door, "There's a machete leaning on the other side of the door."

Cozy Mae grabbed the machete, removing it from its scabbard. "Let's go. Ruth Ann and Sparkle, you stay here with Rodney. We'll call for help if y'all's help is needed."

Sally turned to Rodney. "Rodney, you call Mulriley if I give the word. But wait for me to say it."

"But... but... milady! I forgot the word! You could be dead by the time I find the file to refresh my memory."

Sally rolled her eyes. "Rats! Me, too. Today the word is '*help*'!"

"Got it! I am all over it. *Help*! A word I know well."

Sally and Cozy Mae inched out the door and peeked around the end of the vestibule. "The boots are still there, Coze. Come on. Lock in stealth mode."

Creeping along with their respective weapons raised, both women jumped then raced forward when the foot moved. They stood over him; armed to strike if he moved without permission.

Seeing them, he threw his arms over his face. "Don't hurt me! I'm not here to cause you harm! I came to get back what's mine."

Sally tilted her head and stared at him. Recognition dawned on her...

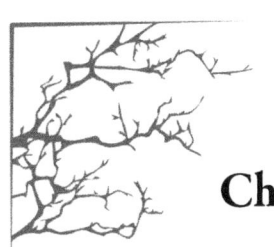

Chapter 17 – Camo Crook

"You're the stupid criminal that got away with about $20 from the laundromat! Why would you come back for more?"

He moved his hands to the palm outward like a stop sign. "May I get up and explain, please?"

Sally shook her head. "No, you may not. You explain from right where you are."

"Okay, okay... Have it your way, lady. I'll tell you. But I need to reach into my shirt pocket to show you why I robbed that store."

Sally and Cozy raised their weapons for immediate action. "Go ahead. Reach," Sally said.

He stuck two fingers in his shirt pocket and brought out a quarter. Handing it to Sally, he said, "That's what I was after when everything went awry."

Sally studied it. It was old... dated 1823. The 3 looked odd – like it was printed in error. Not in great condition, but clear enough to read. "What about it?" She passed it on to Cozy and eyed the villain.

"It's an overdate. I found it the day before in a roll of quarters I opened at my job. I bought it from my drawer – all fair and square.

I work a graveyard shift. Money has been tight. My wife gathered all the quarters she could find and traded them at the local laundry for paper money. This quarter got swept into the mix.

The quarter is worth $35,000. I *had* to have it back.

Granted, I didn't think through the method I used... but it's what I did." He drew in a breath before continuing.

"I was coming to your house for food and water while things cooled down. But by the time I survived your moat and was subjected to your paint-mine, I was mad as a wet hornet and panicked. I stashed the quarter out here before I busted into your house; just in case I got nailed. Which you did very effectively, I might add." He scowled.

"Having done my time and made restitution for the $20, I thought I could sneak in here; retrieve my quarter; and get out without you being any the wiser. I proceeded. And I was in fine shape until my shirt caught on the oven door and falling dominoes happened.

And now here we are again. Please don't hog-tie me and call the cops again. I just wanted my quarter."

Sally tugged her ear, calling on her intuition for discernment. The story was so far-fetched it had to be true. Nobody was harmed. Not even the culprit. He had no visible weapon.

Sally lowered her stick. "Alright. You can get up. Come and grab a stump while I ponder all this." Sally perched on her cushy office chair under the ironwood tree. She waved him to sit. He did.

Sally: "Where do you work?"

Villain: "Nowhere now. I was fired for the conviction."

Sally: "Where did you work before you whomped the girls with a gun?"

Villain: "At the mini-mart."

Sally: "Do you have children?"

Villain, nodding: "Twin girls. Six months old." He smiled.

Sally: "What will you do for work now?"

Villain: "Probably construction... I'll have to be gone a lot..." He shrugged. "But it's the price I will pay forever. I don't see me getting hired if handling money is part of the job. I was working in the mini-mart because my wife was having problems with the pregnancy.

I needed to be home to help her instead of miles and hours away on a roadbuilding job."

Sally eyed Cozy Mae. She smiled back with an ever so slight nod.

THE SCREECHING SHADOWS OF HIDDEN VALLEY

Sally nodded. "Okay. You can go. This is strictly between us forever and ever." She waved him away. "Vamoose now, before I change my mind."

The camo criminal skipped out the lane fast. Sally heard a car engine start a few minutes later.

Rodney appeared at the end of the portico to the igloo. "I did it, Sally. I called Mulriley. He's on his way."

Sally froze. "Why did you call Mulriley? Neither I nor Cozy said '*help*'."

Rodney blinked. "Somebody did. I heard the word. I made the call."

Sally slapped her hand over her mouth. "Oh, my. Call him back fast and tell him it was a misunderstanding... everything is fine."

Rodney bleeped while he made the call. "Too late, milady. He's coming down the lane now. He says he'll have a mugga with you."

Ruth Ann and Sparkle stood next to Rodney. "Can we come out now?" Ruth Ann asked. "Who is Mulriley?"

Sally's shoulders sank. She rocked out of the chair. "Very well, then. I'll get the coffee and cookies. He may as well meet you all."

Ruth Ann grumbled. "But who is Mulriley? Do we love him or hate him?"

Rodney rolled his eyes. "We love him, Ruth Ann. He is the chief detective for this county. He is a good guy who has a crush on Joany. But he never tells her so.

He is also an authority figure. Do not blab about anything more than you are asked about specifically. Do not speak unless spoken to. Got it?"

"I got it," she pouted. "You sure are bossy sometimes, Rodney."

"I am an old man, Ruth Ann. I can be bossy."

Mulriley came around the igloo, whistling Dixie. "Good morning, Sal... Oops! Wait! You're not Sally. I recognize Rodney. What have you done with Sally?"

Cozy Mae chuckled and offered her fist for a bump. "I'm Sally's cousin from Jack County, Texas. She's getting your coffee and cookies. These are my bots, Ruth Ann and Sparkle. Ruth Ann's the girl. Sparkle is the pup. In case you wondered."

He bumped Cozy's fist and hunkered down on a stump. "Usually when I get a call, there's a body somewhere in the mix." He looked around. "But I don't see a body. Was there almost one? Why did you make the call, Rodney?"

Rodney bleeped. "Well, you see..."

Ruth Ann interrupted. "He was supposed to call you if Sally said the word *help*. But it was the guy that was here that said the word *help* when he was talking about his wife. Rodney called you when he should not have."

Mulriley tilted his head toward Ruth Ann. "Oh? There was a guy here talking about his wife who needed help? What was his name?"

Ruth Ann shrugged. "I do not know. Em and Sally snuck up on him with a big stick and a machete. But they did not..."

"Hush, Ruth Ann! You're telling stories out of context..."

Chapter 18 – The Big Mouth

"I am only answering the man's questions, Em. I am doing just what Rodney told me to do... Speaking when spoken to and only blabbing about what I was specifically..."

"Stop talking, Ruth Ann! Now! Let's you and I take a walk. We still have to make our beds in the camper." Cozy stood and took Ruth Ann by the hand. "Come on, Sparkle." The dog followed, wagging his tail.

Sally came out the door with a mug of coffee in one hand and a plate of cookies in the other. "I didn't want you to stop what you were doing unnecessarily, Michael. Rodney misunderstood. He thought he was doing the correct thing, if that counts."

Mulriley smiled at Sally. "It's alright. I was ready for a break on the old home place. And your alien company gave me quite an earful of what's been going on here."

Sally chuckled. "Did she now?"

Mulriley smiled. "That she did. Your cousin did her best to shut her up. But I expect you'll want to expand on and clarify a couple of things, anyway."

Sally fidgeted in her chair. "Oh? Will I?"

He sipped coffee, watching Sally. "Yes. Things like why you needed a big stick and a machete to sneak up behind a guy..." He shrugged. "You know. Things like that."

Sally, with eyebrows raised, "A stick and a machete, you say? Hmm... Oh that." She waved Mulriley away. "Pshaw! It was nothing.

We heard noises in the outdoor kitchen. You know I'm a prepper – right?"

Mulriley nodded, circling with his hand for her to get on with it.

Sally splayed her hand. "Well, Cozy and I went to check out the noises. We went prepared. But it was nothing." She shrugged. "It was as simple as that." She shook her head. "You know how youngsters are. They get things all out of whack sometimes."

Mulriley nodded. "That they do. But what about the fella saying *help* that inspired Rodney to call me?"

Sally rolled her eyes. "Another simple misunderstanding. The guy said he had to help his wife with something... I don't remember what. I'd told Rodney before we went out that *help* is the code word to call you. He heard the word and called you. It just came from the wrong person. But he did exactly as I'd said."

"Hmm." Mulriley rubbed his goatee. "You have an answer to about everything. But who was this guy that started these dominoes falling?"

"Name?" Sally tugged her ear. "I guess I didn't get his name. There was no need."

Mulriley scoffed. "Then what was he here for? Surely you know that."

Sally shook her head. "Not really. He just said he was looking for something he'd lost and thought maybe he'd dropped it here on his earlier trip through."

Mulriley chuckled. "You know we could do this for hours. Me prying; you dancing around my questions. Never giving straight answers."

Sally smiled. "Then I suggest you eat your cookies and drink your coffee, mister. Before I get to feeling like I'm being 3rd degreed."

Now he laughed. "You win, old girl. I can only hope you'd tell me if there was anything going on that I need to know about."

Sally nodded, saying nothing. She picked up her empty mug. "Refill?"

THE SCREECHING SHADOWS OF HIDDEN VALLEY

The subject was closed.

"My turn, Michael. What have you learned about this midnight screecher? And the fires?"

He shook his head. "Not a thing. Nobody sees a thing that they'll talk about. But they sure do want to talk about the inept police department that can't find the culprits. It's frustrating. At least we've been successful with putting out the fires while they're puny. And the neighborhood helps with that." He turned to Sally. "So, you've heard or surmised nothing, either?"

Sally shook her head. "No verifiable conclusions. Only conjecture. But I'll share them with you in case you haven't already gone down my personal rabbit holes." Mulriley grinned and nodded.

Sally continued, "I say it's either," she counted off on her fingers:

- An angry elephant with a Bic in its trunk and a fire-stamping rhino for a sidekick. Or...
- A new scavenger hunt game where the one who's '*it*' has an amped up bullhorn. The player bellows; the rest try to locate the screeching player. When the screecher is found; the finder lights a fire to communicate the find to the rest of the players.

And there ya are." She splayed her hands. "That's the best I got right now. What do you think?"

Mulriley grinned. "I think you have an excellent imagination. But have you researched the new game theory? It sounds outrageous enough to be correct."

Sally shook her head. "Not thoroughly. Rodney was digging into the dark web for such a game. He was interrupted, so hasn't completed his search." She looked at Rodney.

"Or, have you been able to get back to your search, Rodney?"

Rodney bleeped. "What, milady? I was napping. I am starting to feel as old as I look these days. What did you want me to do?"

"I asked if you've been able to complete your search on the dark web for the screeching game we talked about. The search you were interrupted from this morning."

"Oh, that. No, ma'am. I have not gotten back to it. Do you wish me to do that now? It is a very scary place, the dark web."

Chapter 19 – The Search

"If you wouldn't mind, Rodney. But you should go plug in before you dive into it again. You were pretty deep and had trouble getting out this morning. Can you be safe?"

"I hope so. That is all I can say. Get me out of it if I am not back in an hour."

Sally bit her lip and tugged her ear. "Hmm. Maybe you better skip it. I'm sure Michael has dark web techys available that can keep themselves safe."

Mulriley interrupted. "I do." He stood and handed Sally his mug. "Leave it to me, Rodney. Don't put yourself in harm's way again.

I'll get back to you on that one, Sally. But don't hold your breath on proving the angry elephant theory."

Rodney bleeped. "Thank you, sir. It was spine-chilling for little old me."

Mulriley smiled and nodded at Rodney. "Next time, family." He disappeared behind the igloo.

Sally shook her head. "Rodney."

"Yes, milady?"

"Did Mulriley just call us *family*?"

"Let me look... Why, yes, he did."

Sally tugged at her ear. "Puzzling. Very puzzling, that shy Scotch-Irishman who's in love with niece Joany; but hasn't told either himself or her yet."

☺

Cozy Mae came around Sally's igloo from her camper. "Is he gone?"

Sally nodded.

"I tried to get Ruth Ann gone before she spilled the entire pot of beans." She shook her head.

"Good call on the virus search and destroy. She got rid of several viruses last night with deep cleaning. I think she's a little less chatty. But she still has a mouth runneth over issue.

She wants to go find the screecher. She says Sparkle has the coordinates of where the sound came from. She also says that Bro was just opening up to Sparkle when we interrupted their talk. I forget why we interrupted now."

Sally grinned. "I remember. It was to get everybody cleaned up after subjecting them to public Wi-Fi. It's too bad. I'm really curious about Bro's agenda. But he didn't have to leave." She sighed.

"I guess it's not time to get the epilogue on Bro. He's still fun and huggable." She chuckled. "If you'd have seen him take out after those two that grabbed Rodney and Teague. That was the first and only time I've heard him bray – so far."

Cozy cleared her throat. "So, what do you think about going on a screecher hunt? Ruth Ann really wants to go. She's sure we can solve the mystery in one short jaunt."

"Well, why not? Let's load 'em up and go. We'll take my van. That way you can handle your charges and guide us to the place." She stood from her chair. "I'll meet you at the van. Rodney can ride on the bed along with your guys. You can ride shotgun."

Cozy shook her head. "I'll ride on the bed with my guys. That way I can see what they're looking at. It will work more efficiently."

Sally shrugged. "Okay then. Whatever works.

Rodney, have Amy take you to the van. I have to lock up the place and get the keys... in some order."

"Yes, milady. Amy. Take me to the van."

THE SCREECHING SHADOWS OF HIDDEN VALLEY

Sally picked up Rodney to set him in the seat. "Mind the shoes, milady. I would not want to horrify Ruth Ann and Ms Cozy with my gnarly foot."

"Minding the shoes, Rodney. I'll tell them not to look if your shoe comes off. It will be fine. And you came by it while you were trying to be a hero... conquering a wild and crazy cat. You've nothing to be ashamed of."

Rodney blinked. "I know. But the gasping and gawking gives me butterflies in my belly. I do not like the feel of butterflies dodging about in my tummy. It makes me want to throw-up."

Sally laughed. "You silly boy. I'll keep your mashed-up foot hidden. But you're all tucked in now. Shoes in place. Buckled up. You're good to go."

She slammed the side slide door on Cozy Mae and the kids; unlocked the driver's door and used the steering wheel to pull herself up into the seat. The engine started. She counted the clicks to engage the transmission since her gear pointer had disappeared some years ago. Deciding it was one more obstruction to a wannabe thief, she didn't see the urgency in getting it repaired when counting clicks worked just fine..

"And we're off like a herd of turtles. Where are we going, Coze?"

The journey was fraught with gobbledy-gook instructions. Sparkle yipped and whined to Ruth Ann. Ruth Ann then told Cozy Mae. But much got lost in the translation. Sally knew this because they're journey took them from one end of the valley to the other; crossroad-by-crossroad.

Sally giggled each time they zig-zagged to yet another road that made up the Hidden Valley homestead quilt.

About 2 ½ hours later, they arrived at the elusive location 'X'. Sally parked the van off the road. They climbed out.

It was a vacant lot. There was no sign of tire tracks... but giant, 3-toed sasquatch footprints sunk into the virgin desert crust in several places.

Creosote bushes and rabbit brush dotted the landscape. A small patch of scorched chaparral lined the property border. An old adobe house sat to the north of the lot. It looked abandoned. Or, at least, in need of some TLC. There were no close neighbors.

Sally snapped a picture of a footprint with her own foot next to it for comparison. The print made her own foot look like the itty-bittyest little toe in the world. "That is one giant footprint. But is it real? It looks like this guy has only one foot and hops from pillar to post.

Is everybody satisfied that it remains a mystery?"

"I am," Cozy Mae said. "And I'm hungry. Let's go home. Can you find your way, Sally? Or do I need to go through pink-haired Ruth Ann and Sparkle's gibberish again?"

Sally chuckled. "No. I got it. We're about a mile away."

Cozy Mae laughed while she boosted her kidlets into the van. "And there ya are..."

Chapter 20 – Home Again

Everybody piled out of the van – except Rodney. He had to wait for Sally and Amy. "I want to walk, Ms Sally. Ruth Ann and Sparkle can walk. Why cannot I?"

Sally cradled him in her arms to move him from the van seat to Amy. "Oh, Rodney." She sighed. "Dear, dear Rodney. How can you be so intelligent, yet so not knowing?

I will meet you under the ironwood tree and do my best to tell you why. You go ahead while I close up the van and get me a beverage."

"Amy! Take me to Sally's thinking place." Amy rolled Sally's life-size man doll away.

While she locked up the van, Sally searched for the simplest way to explain Rodney's limitations to him – like walking; riding a donkey; or pedaling a bike. No bright ideas came to mind. She will have to wing it and hope for the best.

She stopped by Cozy Mae's camper on her way around the igloo. "Rodney and I will be in conference for a bit. What's on your agenda?"

Cozy held a sandwich in her hand. She finished chewing and swallowed. "I think we're going to take a little nap. We'll see y'all later."

Sally grinned and nodded. "Very good. Later, cuz." Then she trekked off and disappeared around the igloo.

With a mug of coffee and a glass of water, Sally slid into her cushy chair under the ironwood tree. She took a sip from both cups and cleared her throat.

"Okay, Rodney. You got your ears on?"

"Yes, milady."

"Very good. I'll try to give you the nutshell version first. You can then ask me questions from there. Okay?"

"Yes, milady."

She cleared her throat again. "The bare bones answer is that you have no bones – no skeleton to give you structure and strength. You were built by my and my daughter's loving hands as a lark. We never dreamed you would become a life-form.

Your evolution into a mankin was not part of the plan on that day. So... to give you a skeletal system that would support your back and legs – what you need to walk, run, and ride – we would have to totally dissect you and give you a completely new body. You would not be Rodney anymore; but a stranger in my midst. I would grieve for you.

Also, my mankin, it could take months before you would see the light of day again. Reconstructing you entails major surgery. I would need Christopher and Matthew's help. And they don't have much time these days.

Is that what you want? To be in pieces on the work table; missing out on everything until you are put together again..." her words trailed off.

Rodney bleeped. "Hi, Ruth Ann! Do you want to see where the old skeletons were found? Amy. Take me to Ruth Ann and Sparkle."

Sally grinned like the proverbial Cheshire cat; winking her eyebrows along with the smile. And took Rodney's behavior as a solid *'no'* – not today. She breathed relief and turned her mental energies to the screecher.

Grabbing her phone, she had a vague memory of hearing about a screeching, roaring monkey that lives in the forest canopies of Central and South America.

Searching Google for 'sounds that monkeys make', she played a video recorded at the Houston Zoo of Howler Monkeys. She played it again and again, listening for the similarities between the monkey's howl and their screecher.

By the third time through the video Cozy Mae came tromping around the igloo, her eyes wide and forehead creased. "Oh! I thought the screecher had y'all by the short hairs! What are you doing?"

Sally gaped at Cozy Mae. "Sorry. I just remembered that there's a monkey that makes a horrific sound. It's called a howler monkey.

According to the zoo keeper, this is the sound that the monkeys make before dawn... 3-4 AM. She says they make the sound to claim their tree so others won't come calling in it. But I'm undecided about whether that's the sound we're hearing.

The howler monkey is not your run-of-the-mill pet monkey. They're mean and aggressive. And diurnal other than this pre-dawn marking of territory to other howler families. Not nocturnal at all.

What do you think?" She tapped play again. When it finished, Sally tugged her ear and shook her head. "I don't know. This guy doesn't seem screechy enough. But I guess it's possible.

But then, if this is the screecher, how do we explain the footprints?"

Cozy laughed. "Y'all mean that hopping sasquatch amputee? From what ah've seen and heard of big foot, his foot is not *that* big!

And how many toes does big foot have?"

Sally shrugged and giggled. "Maybe he lost two toes when he lost his other leg. The three he had left spread out like bird claws to give him balance. That would be Darwin's answer."

Cozy slapped the air toward Sally. "Now y'all are gettin' in way too deep for me. My dad would be turning over in his grave if he heard us discussing our journey from a fish to an ape to a man."

Sally laughed. "My only question is: if the new form was so great, why do we still have fish and apes? Or are the number of fish in the sea what the warmongers are counting on as their troops to annihilate the rest of us? What will they do with all the land in the world at their beck and call? Won't they run out of fish to evolve and be their slaves?"

ALEXIE LINN

Cozy jiggled while she belly-laughed on her stump until Sally feared she'd fall off. "Stop! I see dad turning red; beginning to boil. He'll whomp us for sure!"

Chapter 21 – Rodney?

Gathering themselves together after their nonsensical laughing spell, Sally peered around, listening for Rodney's officious story telling. She neither heard nor saw any of the three bots. "Have you seen the kids recently, Coze?"

"Hmm. Now that y'all mention it... Please don't let them be into another paintball mine!" She hefted herself off the stump. "I'll sure be glad when my queen-size chair arrives. But now... where are those scamps?"

Sally rocked out of her chair. "I'll get my stick. It must be time for a walk."

They walked the moat for the entire property, spying nothing. Hearing nothing. Sally saw where someone had drug in two long 2"x 12" boards; long enough to bridge the cholla infested moat. Her stomach knotted. "Those boards are not good news, Cozy." She pointed to the mashed grasses. "Somebody has breached the moat successfully. Recently. The chaparral has not had time to stand up again.

Our kidlets have escaped. With help." She growled.

"No. No. No, Sally. That just can't be! Doesn't Rodney know not to leave the property without you?"

Sally nodded. "Yes, he does. But he is Rodney. No matter how hard he tries to obey the rules, he can make grim choices. He has. Many times." Then she saw Amy, sitting alone and empty; on the other side of the moat. "But not this time. Why would Amy be without Rodney sitting in her?"

Sally's phone beeped a message received. She pulled it from her pocket, swiped and tapped to read it.

'*Help! We have been stolen!*' she read, her heart sinking.

"Oh, my... Cozy Mae, hang on to your hat. They've been snatched!" She typed a reply to the text. And read the responding texts to Cozy Mae as they arrived.

'*Where are you?*'

Rodney: '*I do not know. They covered our eyes.*'

Sally: '*What do they want?*'

Rodney: '*Money. I hear them laughing about all the money they will get for us.*'

Sally: '*How much money? When? Where?*'

Rodney: '*I do not know yet. They have not said. They do not know I am talking to you.*'

Sally: '*Hang on. I'm calling Christopher. He can find your GPS signal.*'

Sally punched Christopher's phone listing harder than she intended. He answered on the first ring. Sally never calls without a good reason.

"Yes, Gram. What's up?"

"Rodney's been kidnapped. Can you get his GPS signal fast?"

"What? Somebody stole Rodney? The dummies. I'll find him and text you the coordinates. I'll call you back in a few minutes."

"Thank you." She ended the call. "We may as well trek back to the tree. If they haven't figured out how savvy are guys are, we'll know exactly where they are in a few minutes.

I'll get my keys to the van, my self-defense fanny pack, and give Mulriley a heads-up."

Cozy Mae followed Sally back to the igloo in zombie mode; not uttering a word.

While they waited, Sally asked Cozy Mae why Sparkle did not ray gun them with his eyes.

THE SCREECHING SHADOWS OF HIDDEN VALLEY

"Huh! Ray gun? Sparkle? Oh. He's like a bird. If you cover his eyes, he goes to sleep immediately. That's how I control him. It's the same with Ruth Ann. If her eyes are covered, she's unaware of any danger or reason to be angry. It's a wonder I haven't been arrested yet for child and animal abuse when I have to calm them in public view."

A message received beeped on Sally's phone. "It's the coordinates of where Rodney is. He included a map, thank goodness. Our guys are currently about 2 miles down the road near the county gravel pit. I'll call Mulriley while you button up your house."

"Hi, Michael. Some yahoos stole Rodney and Cozy Mae's bots. Christopher located them by Rodney's GPS. They're down by the county gravel pit. I'll forward you the map.

Cozy Mae and I are leaving now to get them back. Can you come for back-up in case there's trouble?"

"Hang on there, Sally! You chill and wait for me. Have they made any ransom demands?"

"Not yet. According to the texts I got from Rodney, they're talking big bucks for themselves but haven't said how much they were going to demand. They, apparently, aren't very tech savvy because they haven't flipped Rodney's power off yet. I don't want them to discover their faux pas and move our guys."

"Ok, old girl. This is what you're going to do. No arguments!

You go to where you can see the vehicle. You watch and wait for me.

If you see them move, you follow at a safe distance and don't get made. Then call me back with where you are. Do you know the kind of rig they have?"

"No sir. Rodney said they covered their eyes. That's why neither Ruth Ann nor Sparkle turned them into cinders. According to Cozy Mae, covering the bot's eyes puts them to sleep. They are unaware of what's going on."

"You hope," Mulriley grumbled. "I can't see myself charging two young robots with murder – even if it was self-defense."

"I gotta go, Michael. I'll send you the map when I locate them." Sally ended the call and started the engine. "Keep your eyes peeled, Coze. Although without an idea of what kind of vehicle we're looking for...

There's never anybody down here... I hope they stick out like a sore thumb. But we must stay out of sight, too. This will be quite the challenge. Maybe I should have painted my van desert camo instead of gray..."

Cozy cut in, "There's no time for paint jobs now, Sal. Focus! Drive!"

Sally honed in on the road and desert around her. Nothing stuck out. No vehicles were visible. She called Christopher. "Did they move? We should be right on top of them!"

"Hang on, Gram. I'll look." Sally counted off the seconds to keep from babbling into the phone. "Nope. He hasn't moved. I'm at work or I'd come help you. I gotta go. Keep me posted."

A text message came in. *'They threw me out the door. Help!'*

Sally's heart pumped fast and furious while she tried to see a lump of Rodney under the creosotes and rabbit brush.

"A van just flitted across on the other road. It's white. There's an insignia on the door, but I can't make it out." Cozy spit the words out.

Chapter 22 – Ruth Ann!

Sally called Mulriley. "I hope you're close! Cozy just saw a white van with an insignia on the door headed out Liebre road... Hurry!"

"Done!" the detective said.

"Okay, Coze. Mulriley has that covered. But Rodney's GPS says he should be right here." She splayed her hands around the desert. "He messaged me that they threw him out the door. I'll park so we can walk. He has to be close to a roadway to be thrown out rather than drug."

A message came in from Mulriley. *'Not them.'*

She replied, *'We're walking the road looking for Rodney.'*

Another message came to Sally's phone. *'$50,000 cash in used small bills to get the bots back. You have 4-hours.'*

Sally handed the phone to Cozy Mae. "Here's your ransom note."

Cozy's jaw dropped. Her head slowly shook 'no'. "It's impossible." She shrugged. "My bank is in Texas. I can't lay my hands on that much cash in 4 hours." Her head shook. "No. I can't do it. My babies are gone forever." Tears ran down her cheeks. She sniffed, reaching in her pocket for a tissue.

Sally peered around for a lump with an orange sweater and designer high-tops; unsure of how to help Cozy Mae when her own belly was churning like a cement mixer.

Then something glinted in the afternoon sun. She grabbed Cozy's arm. "Come on! I think I see him... or at least those silly designer shoes he insisted he have." She picked up the pace; almost dragging Cozy. The distraught cousin followed her as if she was in a trance.

"Rodney! Is that you? Call out!"

"Yes, milady. You have come for me. Just like I knew you would. Oh, Sally. My Sally." He groaned.

Sally saw the orange sweater he loved and wore too often. It was like a security blanket to him. She yanked off the black burlap bag that covered his head. He blinked several times against the sun that bore into his eyes.

"Oh, Sally! I see you! I was suffocating in that head cover! Thank you! Please take me home. It was awful! They threw us into an old white van. It smelled of dirty laundry and rotting food. Have you found Ruth Ann and Sparkle?"

Sally gathered Rodney into her arms. "You have only one shoe, Rodney. Where is your other shoe?"

"I think I lost it when they threw me out of the van. I am sorry, Ms Cozy that you have to see my scarred foot."

Sally admonished Rodney. "Cozy is overwrought about Ruth Ann and Sparkle. She is not the least bit concerned about your war-wounded foot. You have to help us find the kids." It was further to the van than Sally realized. While Rodney is not heavy, per se, he is an awkward load in her arms. Breathing heavy, she said, "Cozy Mae! Help, please!"

Cozy grabbed Rodney and tossed him over her shoulder like a sack of peanuts. He 'Oomphed' like the wind was knocked out of him. His remaining shoe dropped. Sally retrieved it; though she wasn't sure why. Will they stumble on to the other one? Why didn't they find it before they found Rodney? Is it still in the stinky van?"

With Rodney sprawled on the bed in her own van, Sally gave him the 3rd degree. "We need clues, Rodney. Playback your files as they are – no editing." She texted Mulriley.

'We got Rodney. Old white van he says. Smells of dirty laundry and rotting food.'

The detective returned a thumb-up.

THE SCREECHING SHADOWS OF HIDDEN VALLEY

Sally tried to tune her ear to the sounds of the recording. They were definitely talking about how they were going to spend their loot. And that Mexico was their destination after they get the ransom. One voice was familiar. Sally searched her memory for where she'd heard it before.

Cozy said, "I know that voice!" She shook her index finger like it was on the tip of her tongue. "The guy in the kitchen... with the coin..."

Sally felt prickles over her entire body. Her face turned red. "We didn't get his name, Coze. Because he conned us good. We let him go and I didn't tell Michael about him." She shook her head. "That stinker!

He got us, but he underestimated what happens when you mess with Sally." She nodded, grinning. "We'll get him. Actually, he'll get himself. That's how it always seems to work. Rest assured; we'll get your kids back. And he is doomed by his own hand."

She fired up the engine. "Save that, Rodney. We're going to need to hear it again. And Mulriley might need a copy." Counting the clicks with the shifter; she put the van in gear and headed for home.

"Not to worry, cuz. We'll get it figured out. If you'll take Rodney out to retrieve Amy and listen again to the recording, I'll call Mulriley and fill him in on who he's looking for. But I won't fess up to our blunder unless I have to.

How long have we got?"

Cozy looked at her watch. "About 3 ¼ hours."

Sally parked the van, nodding acknowledgement. "I'll see you in a few."

Cozy Mae reached in through the sliding door of the van. She grabbed Rodney by the arm; plucked him off the bed and threw him over her shoulder again.

He yowled a proper "Oomph!" and reminded her to mind the shoe. Sally heard him explaining how they were enticed to cross the moat by the kidnappers. Sally shooed his words aside for the moment while she trekked into the igloo to call Mulriley.

Chapter 23 – The Half-Story

The detective answered. "Yes, Sally."

"I have news and a ransom note. I forwarded you the note. The news is that Rodney has a recording of the event before they threw him out of the van.

There's three of them. I recognized a voice on the recording. It's the fella that robbed the laundry and wound up here on my floor covered in cholla spines and paintball-mine splats."

Mulriley coughed. "He just got out of jail 2-days ago! What a twit! What else?"

"They are arrogantly gleeful about spending their wad in Mexico after they collect the ransom. And discussing where they'll sell Ruth Ann and Sparkle if they don't get the money from us.

It seems they threw Rodney out because one of them heard him bleep while he was recording or texting me. They couldn't find an 'off' button so they tossed him out the door on Robles Road. And one of his shoes is missing. He's all in a dither about his designer high-top."

The detective cleared his throat. "All my available deputies are out cruising the roads, looking for the van. The culprits will stay close until they get the cash – or know it's not going to happen. So, there was no clue on the recording of how they're going to collect the ransom?"

Sally shook her head. "Not that I heard the first time through the recording. Rodney and Cozy Mae are retrieving Amy from where they grabbed them. They will be back shortly if you want me to listen again while we're on the phone.

THE SCREECHING SHADOWS OF HIDDEN VALLEY

That dimwit mentioned that this would have been unnecessary if that coin dealer had only given him the full $37,000 for the overdate quarter he robbed the laundry to retrieve."

"Quarter?" Richard asked. "He robbed the laundry for a quarter?"

"Oh. Well." Sally slapped her hand over her mouth and tried not to stammer while she recovered from the slip. "That's what he said on the recording. You can listen for yourself. I told Rodney you'd need a copy made."

"All this for a quarter..." Mulriley muttered. "Unbelievable."

"A quarter, apparently, worth $37,000, fella."

"Humph. Maybe I should take up numismatics in my spare time... if I had any.

But for today, we'll continue to be on the look-out for the van. I'll make it an APB to the entire police force in Pinal County – now that I have a name and rough van description.

Call or text me when you get anything else. If we haven't nailed them by the time they want to collect the ransom, we'll have a plan to grab them at that time."

"Just one more thing, Michael."

"Yes, Sally?"

"Do you know about Ruth Ann and Sparkle's ray-gun eyes?"

Mulriley chuckled. "Their what? Ray-gun eyes, you say?"

Sally sighed. "I know. It sounds ludicrous. Beyond imagining. But Cozy Mae's husband was an inventor of great caliber. He built them to be companions and protectors.

He installed ray-guns behind their eyes. If they get enraged or terror-stricken, they vaporize the source of the threat."

He laughed. "You're spoofing me, old woman."

"Sadly, I'm not. I've seen Sparkle in action. And, apparently, Ruth Ann's hair turns bright red before she fires. Although I haven't seen her hair turn bright red yet."

Now the detective was cracking up. "I don't know what you're drinking or smoking, Sally... but I'll be careful not to provoke either one of them before I call out the crazy lady police on you." He was silent for a moment.

"So, if they shoot first and ask questions later, how come they haven't turned their captors into ash?"

"Cozy says they go to sleep instantly when their eyes are covered. Like hawks. And Rodney said they covered their heads before they grabbed them.

It will all be over if they remove the covers from their eyes."

Giggles continued to escape from Mulriley. "Okay then. I'm giving you the benefit of the doubt. Because I know the kind of crazies you attract.

We'll continue to patrol until it's time to hand over the cash. I might send Deputy Regent to the station to prepare a ransom packet like we did before.

We'll get them, Sally. Assure your cousin of that. You know how we operate. And, so far, we've always got our man... or woman."

Sally heaved a sigh. "I know you will. I'll tell her. But they're her legacy from her late husband. She's very fretful. And I don't blame her. Her kids are being held hostage. She's powerless to fix it."

"Later, Sally. I see an old white van parked alongside the road ahead of me." The call ended.

Amy came through the door with Rodney on board. Cozy Mae followed.

"Good. I'm glad both Amy and Rodney are functioning properly. I won't ask how you are holding up. I had quite a long talk with Detective Mulriley." She waved toward the thermos. "You ready for coffee? I am."

"I think tea, if y'all don't mind." She stood. "I'll get it. Y'all stay put and tell all." She carried the cookie jar and two paper towels over to the table while she waited for the water to boil.

THE SCREECHING SHADOWS OF HIDDEN VALLEY

"I told him the voice on the recording was the same as the guy that robbed the laundry. And that they are headed for Mexico when they finish this caper.

I told him about the van.

He's put out an all-points bulletin on the guy and the van. Deputy Regent... you'll like her... she's cool and fun and formidable. She's putting together a ransom packet in case we need it. But he spotted an old white van parked alongside the road as we were talking. Maybe he's got them already.

I told him about their ray-gun eyes. He's still laughing but says he will be very careful." Sally pulled a cookie from the jar and crunched a bite. "And now I want to know how this all went down, *Sir* Rodney, who knows to not leave the compound without me."

Her phone beeped a message received. She opened it. '*Van was empty. Except for Rodney's shoe.*'

Chapter 24 – The BOLO

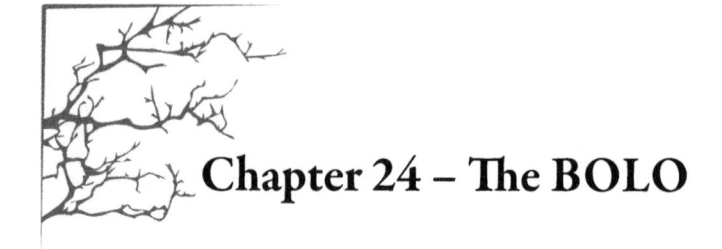

"Rats! Rats! Rats! Cozy. The van was empty... except for Rodney's high-top. It *was* the correct vehicle. *Was* being the operative word." Sally made a fist. "Looks like I've underestimated them as well. Bummer!

But we'll get 'em, Cozy. Know it. Let's listen again to Rodney's recording. There has to be more clues in it." She perched on the arm of the recliner, facing Rodney's corner.

"All right, Rodney. You've bought more time to come up with a believable story of how you all got nabbed. We need to hear the record again."

"Yes, milady. Playing the record."

The conversation was in bits and pieces; caused by the radio and other background noise. Cozy and Sally directed their ears to pick up on each word spoken.

Aside from what they'd already reported; they heard a reference to the abandoned fueling station on the 8. Sally knew it. It was a fally-down adobe right next to the highway. The only way to access it was by way of the Freeman exit. The ruins sat like 5-feet from the interstate. Very visible. It had no garage or even any complete walls to hide a vehicle behind. The logic wasn't there, but whoever accused kidnappers of being logical?

"Stop the record, Rodney. I need to text Mulriley about that old adobe station – or what's left of it."

"Stopping the record, milady."

The response? '*Heh, heh. Got it.*'

THE SCREECHING SHADOWS OF HIDDEN VALLEY

Cozy wrung her hands. "I need some bread dough to knead, or something. I'm feeling culture shock on top of worry. I miss the chaos of 37 big and little people to care for daily."

Sally waved toward the kitchenette. "Have at it. But 18-loaves at a pop is a little overkill. Can you cut your recipe down to one or two loaves?"

Cozy chuckled and rattled pans while Sally tuned her ear to the rest of the recording. Including the end when Rodney's live action was discovered. Here's how it went...

'Did you hear that?'

"No, bro. What the ... you talking about?'

'The old guy doll! He blipped or bleeped or something. I don't see anywhere to shut him down. He's not like the other two. He's like... old school. He could be sending a signal of some sort.'

'Throw him out, dude. He won't bring more than a few dollars, anyway.'

The sound of a sliding door opening; an 'oomph' when Rodney landed; a slam when the door was closed; and an idling engine fading as it got farther and farther away.

The recording ended; Rodney's wrath did not.

"Did you hear that, Ms Sally? He called me *old school* and an *old man doll*! And said I will not bring more than a few dollars! I want to punch him right in the kisser with my bionic arm!

And did you notice how I kept my cool to stay with Ruth Ann and Sparkle. I was hoping they would remove the bag from my head so I could snap pictures of them and where we were. But then that *burp* escaped and you heard what happened."

Sally patted Rodney's arm. "It's okay. I know you did your best to protect Ruth Ann and Sparkle. But I want to know how they grabbed you. Did you three cross over the moat on your own?"

Rodney bleeped. "Well, hmm. Kinda. We saw these two boards strung over the moat. I thought maybe you put them there for us to use while we searched for clues to the screecher. We wanted to see what was on the other side. We did.

That's when they came from behind. They covered our heads and swooped all three of us up. They tossed us in the van... I knew it was a van from the sound of the sliding door. I saw a flash of white just before everything went black.

It was a bumpy ride in the beginning. Then it smoothed out and I started recording. If only I had not burped!"

"I know, Rodney. I know. But we can't go back and relive it to change the outcome. And I didn't hear anything on the recording to help find them. And now they've changed vehicles, anyway.

I'm just relieved they didn't tear you from limb to limb when they discovered you were awake."

"Ouch! That would have really, really hurt Ms Sally. Even more than when Spaghettio ripped my foot to shreds. Eeew... Talk about something else. I can feel the pain."

Sally laughed. "You're such a card, Rodney."

Rodney bleeped. "*Card – Oddball; jester; jokester; zany; humorist.* I guess that is better than being called *old school* and *man doll*. I can be funny."

Sally's phone beeped a message received. It was from the detective. '*Nothing at Freeman.*'

"Bummer," Sally muttered.

"What was that?" Cozy asked, pounding and tossing bread dough around on the countertop.

"He says nothing at Freeman. So... nothing about nothing."

THE SCREECHING SHADOWS OF HIDDEN VALLEY

The bread slammed the countertop with a '*bang!*'. Sally wondered if the countertop will survive. But she decided it wasn't worth mentioning. Cozy's exasperation could be manifesting in a worse way. Several worse ways when you think about it. Images of furniture flying out doors; cars smashing into objects like it was a demolition derby; and glass breaking invaded her mind. She shook it off and brought her attention back to Rodney and his ordeal. The ordeal that is not yet finished to anybody's satisfaction.

Another beep for yet another message arriving lit up Sally's phone. It was from the kidnappers.

'*Bring the $ to the corner of Robles and Almendra Roads at 4 PM sharp! Come alone or the bots go on the auction block tonight.*'

Chapter 25 – The Payoff

"Y'all are *not* going alone, Sally! They're my kids... my responsibility. Your detective is already covering the payoff until I can replace it for him. Don't *even* think about meeting those twerps alone! I'll knock y'all down and sit on ya! Then a'll truss you up like a Thanksgiving turkey ready for the oven if I have to!"

Sally gave Cozy Mae the two-arm slow down signal. "Chill, Cozy! I hear you! And I'm not a martyr! But we have to find a way to stuff your big, beautiful body into the back of my van so that not a hair on your head is visible. Your family is at stake, here, woman. They're more important than your pride, I say."

Sally had already updated detective Mulriley. The women were waiting on him to bring the cash and give them the plan of action. The bread dough Cozy had needed to knead was wrapped in plastic wrap and in the fridge to raise and bake later.

Countryside visibility from that specific corner covered miles and miles. There was no way to hide a police force in plain sight. Sally noted that these villains seemed to be better at this than she first thought.

"ATV coming, milady."

Sally peered out the kitchenette window that faces the parking area. It was detective Mulriley in his undercover garb. He wore farmer john overalls, a plaid shirt, barn boots, and a straw hat.

He sashayed in the door; reached behind the overall bib and dropped a fat envelope onto the table.

"There's your ransom if you have to use it." He pulled a paper out. "Just sign for it here."

THE SCREECHING SHADOWS OF HIDDEN VALLEY

Sally signed. He folded the sheet of paper and stuffed it back inside the bib.

"We'll be everywhere with various farm equipment so we're part of the landscape. Our chase vehicles are stashed close by. Know that we can see you... and them. Call me when you turn onto Almendra and leave the connection open so I can hear what's going down." He turned and sashayed out the door again without a *'hello'*; *'goodbye'*; *'be safe'*; or *'any questions'* muttered.

The big hand on Sally's cow clock edged closer and closer to the hour. Cozy Mae said, "I'm going to take a nap on y'alls bed in the van. Toss blankets and clothing over me like you're in the middle of folding the laundry. A'll find me an airhole to breath and listen. And a'll have my colt 45 cocked and ready."

She tromped out the door. Sally heard the van door slide open and closed.

"Okay, Rodney. Take care of the ranch. I won't be gone any longer than I have to. I'll leave the door open for you in case you have to escape. Do you want the paintball gun armed and ready to fire? You'll have to be very careful that it doesn't go off accidentally."

"No, milady. I want to go outside now before you give me the paintball gun. But yes, I want it. Amy. Take me outside."

"Okay then. I'll bring it for you and set you up on my way out." She looked at the clock. "That would be now."

Sally parked the van off to the side at the specified corner. Another vehicle came toward her, but that's all she could see for activity. She held the envelope of cash in one hand, and her stun-gun in the other. It whirred when she flipped the switch to arm it.

The other vehicle, a blue panel van pulled off on the opposite side of the corner. A hooded man stepped out the door. She opened her door and slid out. She held the bulging envelope so it was visible. The stun-gun remained palmed at her side – invisible.

He pointed at the envelope. "That the cash?"

She nodded. "Bring the bots out."

He shook his head. "Not til I see the cash."

Sally opened the envelope and flashed bills. He reached for it. She jerked the envelope back out of reach. "Not til I see the bots."

Two more hooded guys opened the back doors and lifted Ruth Ann and Sparkle out. The bots' heads were covered with hoods. "Wow! There must have been a sale on black burlap hoods that day," came out of her mouth.

The scoundrel reached again for the envelope. Sally shook her head. "Nope. Take off their hoods. I want to see that they're not damaged."

"Listen, lady! Quit being so obstinate! Give me the envelope and you get the bots!"

"No! Remove their hoods! Then you get the money."

The two villains that held Ruth Ann and Sparkle plucked the black burlap heads off their heads; rolling their eyes and snarling. Sally yelled 'Danger! Danger! They're going to hurt your Em."

The following happened all at once in a matter of seconds.

Ruth Ann's hair turned bright red. She turned her head to the guy that held her and ray-gunned him. He screamed and fell to the ground. Sparkle ray-gunned the guy that held him. He screamed and fell to the ground.

Sally raised her arm and held the stun-gun on the one with his hand out for the money. He screamed and fell to the ground.

Then all you-know-what broke loose with Cozy Mae cannonballing out of the van and police converging from all directions on various farm equipment. Not even one resembled a policeman or woman in dress or their mode of transportation.

Cozy Mae gathered up her babes in her arms and hugged the stuffins out of them. She carried them to the van and sunk into the doorway; rocking them.

Patrol cars zoomed in to cart away the hijackers and their backup blue panel van.

THE SCREECHING SHADOWS OF HIDDEN VALLEY

Sally handed detective Mulriley the fat cash envelope. He returned the signed receipt to her. She tore it into pieces and crammed it in her pocket to secure it until she could get home and burn it.

"Another job well done, old girl," he said, laughing. "Not a bullet was fired. And nobody died. Who could ask for anything more?"

Sally laughed, "How's about solving the screeching pyromaniac issue? Have you gotten anywhere with that?"

"According to Deputy Regent, that van we just confiscated may hold some pertinent clues."

Chapter 26 – The Blue Van

"B-r-r-i-n-g, b-r-r-i-n-g." Sally's phone rang soon after returning home with Cozy Mae and her bots. It was Mulriley. Sally swiped and tapped to answer his call.

"Yes, Michael."

"We may have hit paydirt in the blue van. We've found an amplified megaphone and recordings inside. They're playing the records now to see what's on them. But the game you suggested may be what's going on. That's why I'm sharing this with you. Although it may be premature... there's been no screeching roars yet. I'll get back to you, Sally." The call ended.

Cozy Mae came into the igloo; Ruth Ann and Sparkle trailing her closely. "It's decided, Sally. We're going home and restart our adventure after we've had time to heal from this one." She shook her head. "Between the screecher and the kidnapping, I need to get back to baking 18 loaves of bread at a time and familiar unevents for a bit. I hope you understand."

"Pshaw, girl. I not only understand it, I've lived it. You absolutely need to do what your heart tells you to do. But are you leaving tonight?"

Cozy shook her head. "No, ma'am. But soon. I hope this screecher mystery gets solved and that Sparkle can converse with Bro to share his agenda. I've never heard of anything so weird as that donkey's behavior with you."

"Oh." Sally slapped her fingers to her chin. "You could drag the tiny donkey trailer back with you if you'd like. I can't imagine that I'd be needing it again. Bro seems to be exactly where he wants to be."

Cozy Mae tapped her temple with her finger. "Let me just think about that. I don't think we need it back there, either." She shook her finger aimed at the ceiling. "I'll talk with somebody about it. I don't know who's on the schedule for what department this week. I'll get back to you on that."

Cozy Mae laughed. "I don't know if it's good news or bad news that they can run the entire outfit and their own lives without me. I feel relief and shoved out of the nest at the same time. It seems like at least one of them should need something from me..." her words trailed off.

"Stop that, Cozy Mae Thorne! It just means you've done a great job of parenting and managing. Remember that they're adjusting and grieving, too. They're giving you space and unraveling ties. Just as they should. Stay in the middle of that spiral, Cozy girl. Don't head down it. Just ride it out and let life happen heading upward slowly.

And now I'm done preaching. I'll shove this soapbox under the bed. And remind you that niece Joany is at the ready if you need some help. She's very good at what she does."

Sally stood with her hands on her hips in her inherited grandma pose. "What's for supper? We've had a long, long traumatic day. If Mulriley's hunch is right, the screecher has been corralled and we can sleep without interruptions tonight."

Cozy Mae laughed. "Finger food that doesn't make any dirty dishes." She snapped her fingers. "I forgot that I have bread dough in the refrigerator. I'll set it to rise. We can luxuriate in fresh bread and jam for supper." She went to the fridge; removed the dough; shaped it and flopped it in a pan.

She lit the burner to warm it, then shut off the flame; plopped the pan on it with a towel over the top. "There! It'll be ready for the oven in about 20 minutes. Does that work for you?"

Sally nodded. "Absolutely! You go, girl!"

With Rodney's missing shoe retrieved from the detective, Sally put them back on his feet. He had nothing to report while Sally was gone. But he was adamant that he, Ruth Ann and Sparkle could be trusted to go outside and share horror stories of the day.

Sally shivered. "Okay, but do not cross the moat or leave the property – no matter how tempting it is! And watch for paintball mines!" She shook her head." On second thought, stay right around here under the ironwood or mesquite tree. Don't go beyond the water tanks."

Rodney blinked his out of sync eyes fast and scoffed. "But Ms Sally!"

Sally shook her head. "No, Rodney. No more surprises today! Stay close." She smiled. "But have fun."

An hour later, Sally and Cozy sat drooling at the aroma of fresh out of the oven bread; willing it to cool enough to slice and melt butter.

Cozy touched Sally's hand. "I've enjoyed our time together, cousin. Although I could have done without a couple of highly traumatizing moments."

Sally laughed. "Me, too. What you said. It's always preferred to have a partner in crime, so to speak. I was doing fine without Rodney. Until I got him. Now I'd be sad without him around. I don't know if I like it or dislike it... but there it is."

Cozy laughed. "I know. I seem to need somebody to care for... to gather into my arms and hug the stuffins out of. But I don't need to wash their dirty dishes or do their laundry. My needs stop at hugs and generally looking out for."

"Ms Sally! Ms Sally!" Rodney came racing Amy into the igloo. "Ms Sally! Come and see!"

"Come and see what, Rodney?"

"You will not believe it! Come and see!"

THE SCREECHING SHADOWS OF HIDDEN VALLEY

Sally rolled her eyes and looked at Cozy Mae. "You may as well come, too. He's certainly excited about something."

The women followed Rodney out the door and to the end of the vestibule... Their jaws dropped...

Chapter 27 – Close Your Mouth!

Bro stepped up to Sally and nuzzled her neck, leaving his muzzle perched on her shoulder. She wrapped her arms around his neck.

Behind him were two babes in waiting (that looked a lot like Bro, but younger), and an older jack and jenny. Bringing up the rear was two draft mules. They looked to be twin – same size, same coloring, etc. – Belgian draft mules.

"See, Sally? Bro brought us a donkey party!"

Sally took Bro's cheeks in her hands and looked him in the eye. "Have you stolen a donkey family? Is this *your* family? Did some yahoo steal your folks and bring them to Arizona? Is that what your story is? How did you know they were here? Were they up at the wildlife sanctuary? Your entire family?" She shook her head. "How could this happen? How could you have known how to find them... beginning with me?"

Sally went from donkey to donkey and mule to mule, introducing herself and giving them a solid hug. They each nuzzled her while she hugged.

After she'd greeted all the donkeys and mules, she returned to Bro. "Did you have permission to bring your family to my house? Or, is there an all-points bulletin out on you as a donkey and mule thief?" She shook her head. "You can't hide them here. My place is way too visible and active to be safe. You'll get us all sent to the hoosgow.

And those gorgeous draft mules... they have to be worth a fortune in someone's pocket. You'll – or I – will be arrested for grand larceny.

THE SCREECHING SHADOWS OF HIDDEN VALLEY

Or are you here to say farewell because you're headed out with your family to a happy donkey haven?"

She looked at Sparkle. Ruth Ann and Sparkle stepped up. "Can you help me understand, Sparkle?"

Sparkle and Bro carried on a weird and wild conversation for a time. Sparkle then shared the conversation with Ruth Ann.

Ruth Ann stepped up to the podium. She cleared her throat. "Bro says you are correct, Ms Sally. They are headed out to the Alamo Lake and Wikiup area where burros roam freely and there's food and water aplenty.

Bro's dad says he will not be corralled with a monster horse and be expected to impregnate her on demand. While he does not mind accommodating the horse, he does not want to be ordered to perform with another.

Bro says it will take them substantial time to get there because they will have to skirt around the cities and lay low in the daytime so as to not get caught again. And not get mowed down while crossing the freeways.

The mules are Bro's half siblings. And, yes, their mother is a Belgian draft horse. Her caregiver keeps her working, showing, and pregnant with no break. She has no time or energy for the twins.

They want to stay with their dad and choose who they work for; not have their futures chosen for them. They have heard of too many maniacs hurting others. They want no part of it. And they want to work together; not be separated.

Bro also says he does not know how he knew that Sally was the key to be reunited with his family. He just did. And for her not to worry her little gray head about it. Accept it.

He wants Sally to know how much she means to him for stepping up and fulfilling his needs. He will never forget her and will give her a hug anytime their paths cross in the future.

And, finally, he says they will hang out here until dark so they can slip away under the cover of night. And he trusts everybody here to know nothing about their visit, especially Ruth Ann." She slapped her hand over her mouth. "Wait! That's me!" Her hair flashed shades of pink like a strobing emergency lamp.

"Wow!" is all Sally could say. She was mesmerized by the elegant stance and coloring of the Belgian mules. The desire to hop on and go with them to the happy donkey land was overwhelming.

Rodney broke her dreamy journey with, "I will begin filling water buckets, milady. They will need to leave with a full supply of food and water."

Sally nodded. "Good thinking, Rodney."

"Amy. Take me to the water tanks. Follow me, Bro and family."

The herd trod slowly behind Rodney; lining up for the water bucket and heading out to graze. Sally hoped they were smart enough to steer clear of the paintball-mines. A horrific image of orangey/yellow fluorescent blobs of paint fringing these gorgeous equines made her frown. '*But I'm not in control of any of this,*' she reminded herself.

Sally remembered reading somewhere that mules are champion self-preservationists. And donkeys are more narcissistic than horses as well. That's only good news when you are taking on nature's bounty of food and hazards. She prayed that would keep them from setting off a paintball mine while they grazed.

She perched on a stack of bricks under the mesquite tree to etch this final meeting permanently in her memory. She also snapped a photo or two with her phone. Not that she doesn't trust her memory...

Her emotions bounced from sad that Bro is leaving to glad that she was able to play an integral part in fulfilling his desire to join his family. Weepy that he won't be sauntering in to nuzzle and hug her; to joy that he and his family are setting themselves free to roam and choose for themselves.

THE SCREECHING SHADOWS OF HIDDEN VALLEY

She stood from her stack of bricks and trudged among them, petting and hugging each steed time and time again. She popped into the igloo and raided the fridge for a clutch of carrots. Slicing them into chompable chunks, she stuffed them into her pockets.

Returning to the pasture, she strode among the proud equines again. But this time sharing a treat from her pocket as well as getting another hug and nuzzle.

In her head she was planning a long-term campout near Bagdad, Alamo Lake, and Burro Creek. She was also checking out land for sale in that area. Will it be her new happy hunting ground?

"Soup's on, cousin," Cozy Mae called from the bunny picnic ground. "Come and eat. The shadows are gettin' long."

Sally said her final farewells to the herd of equines. She forced herself to partake of the chicken rice soup that Cozy had served up. Doing her best to shake off the heaviness that had settled onto her like a ton of bricks.

She tucked Rodney in and climbed into her own bed. Throughout the night she found herself a piece of ground near Alamo Lake and homesteaded it. And they all lived happily ever after.

After the rude awakening of the chronic screecher at 2 AM and daylight came, Sally peered out the windows. The compound was vacant of donkeys and mules as if she'd dreamed the whole affair. She booted the computer.

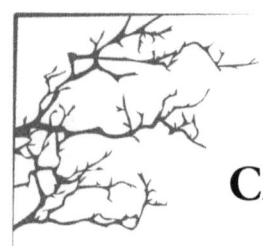

Chapter 28 – Hello Screech

'*He's still here,*' Sally texted Mulriley. '*So much for that theory.*'

'*Yep.*' Is all he replied with.

Cozy Mae came to fill her coffee mug and share Sally's kettle of cornmeal mush.

Spooning in a gob of mush, Sally eyed Cozy Mae. "Tell me I didn't dream that Bro came with his family. And that Sparkle and Ruth Ann interpreted his story."

Cozy shook her head, chasing the gruel with coffee. "You didn't. It happened. His story was moving, to say the least. I hope they're safe and well. Those Belgian mules were magnificent. I can see myself being a hostess for a team of them."

Sally smiled. "Good. I'd hate to think it wasn't real." She slapped her forehead with the heel of her hand. "Duh..." Grabbing her phone, she tapped on the gallery icon. "Here they are. I got pictures."

Cozy took the phone and grinned at the image. "Oh yes... there they are... so perfectly awesome!"

Shoving another spoonful of mush into her mouth and swallowing, she shared her morning's adventure with Cozy Mae. "I found a chunk of land I want to go look at. In the path of where they're headed."

Cozy's eyes grew as big as saucers. Her forehead crinkled. "Y'all are kidding!"

Sally shook her head. "Not! You wanna go check it out?"

THE SCREECHING SHADOWS OF HIDDEN VALLEY

Cozy Mae tilted her head and peered at the sky, as if there was no ceiling to block the view. "Hmm. Maybe. But I'm still going home, cousin."

Sally laughed. "I didn't say you can't go home, silly. I asked if you want to join me on an adventure. It's a yes or no question."

Cozy chuckled. "And I have a *maybe* answer. When do y'all plan to make this excursion?"

"Soon," Sally drained her coffee mug and licked her lips. "I need to gather information on properties and talk to agents to set up viewings. I know I can expect an onslaught of dings from hungry real estate agents. But I don't know any other way to get it done. It's not like I can go hang out in the area and hope someone begs me to take their perfect parcel off their hands."

"What about water?" Cozy shot questions at Sally. "And power? Or are y'all just going to go plop in the middle of it and hope Bro will see to yer needs?"

Sally frowned. "That was a little catty, Coze. It makes me think it's time for us to part company. When are you leaving?"

"Oh, my goodness, Sally. I don't believe I said that. And especially in that tone." Cozy Mae shook her head. "I apologize. I don't know where it came from... so I can't say it won't happen again.

I *can* say that it's never happened before. And I *hope* it never happens again. Do you wish me to go today? Right now?"

"Hmm. Let me ponder that a bit." Sally refilled her mug and replayed Cozy's sorrowful words in her head. She joined Cozy Mae at the table.

"I would hate for us to become strangers again when we just found each other. But I can't live in fear that you are going to verbally attack me. Walking on eggshells is not my way at 87-years-old.

Here's what I suggest if you want to hear it."

Cozy Mae sat up straight and faced Sally. "I will listen."

"I suggest that you meet with niece Joany. I say again that she is very good at what she does.

After you meet with her, you decide whether to stay and play or to leave."

Cozy Mae nodded slowly, winding and unwinding strands of wayward hair. "I will meet with her, Sally. I want to like the old widow lady I'm turning into. Please call her."

Sally picked up her phone and tapped Joany's listing. She did not punch the speaker button.

"Hi Joany. Do you have time to come and visit with cousin Cozy Mae? She's having some grief issues that she's unhappy with." Sally listened with the phone to her ear.

"Good. The coffee's on. See you in a few." She ended the call. "She's on her way. You'll like her."

It wasn't 5-minutes before Sally heard Joany's old creampuff Chevy truck rumbling down the lane. Sally and Cozy Mae walked out the door to meet her.

Sally did the introductions and suggested settling in under the ironwood tree. "I'll go get your coffee, Joany, and leave you two to your business." Joan Freed, Sally's rebel life coach niece, nodded agreement.

Sally booted her computer and made notes on available land parcels in the Alamo Lake to Burro Creek stretch of desert.

With phone calls made, she sat her list of possibilities aside and caught Rodney up on her plans.

"This is exciting, milady! Yes, let's have an adventure and check out new digs near Bro and his family! I hope they discover us soon.

Where will we camp? What do we need to take with us to keep me charged up? How long will we be gone? Should I connect with my brother Teague and Madeline? Shall we invite them to join us in our new life?"

Sally waved at him to slow down. "We're in the beginning stages of thoughts, old man. Keep your shirt on.

THE SCREECHING SHADOWS OF HIDDEN VALLEY

You could check the weather for the next couple of weeks. And the weather in the area in general. We don't need any hotter than here for summer. And winters have to still be relatively mild. I'm not into keeping a fire 24/7 or digging out snow.

Even I have my limits on what I will do for the cause."

Chapter 29 – Joany and Cozy

Sally put the breakfast kettle and utensils away before she stepped outside to see how Cozy Mae and Joany's visit was progressing. But the bunny picnic area was vacant of humans. She assumed they took a hike to the mountain. It seems the mountain – or the hike to it and back – is where a gazillion life-changing decisions are made.

She smiled, happy for the alone time in her cushy repurposed office chair with the birds and bunnies. Ms Lizzy perched on her favorite hunting stand – a rock – for her own breakfast of ants and flies.

Sally began rethinking her whim of moving to commune with the burros. Bro certainly doesn't need her. He and his family will be busy living life to the fullest as free donkeys and mules. Sure, he'd be glad to see her as they passed through. But he doesn't want... or need... to live with her. His agenda is clear now that it's been shared successfully.

Now she is sorry she'd mentioned the idea to Rodney. He'll whine and cry if she doesn't follow through with the adventure of seeking new digs.

She heard niece Joany and Cozy Mae chattering while they returned to Sally's compound. Will Cozy be staying on or heading out? Will Sally be seeking familiar solace or staying put?

The group came around the igloo. Sally called out to Rodney that Ruth Ann and Sparkle are here. He appeared at the end of the portico. The bots wandered away from the picnic grounds. Sally heard Rodney expounding on the possibility of moving to where the donkeys roam free. A ball formed in the pit of her stomach.

THE SCREECHING SHADOWS OF HIDDEN VALLEY

Sally greeted the women. "Hello ladies. What's the good word? Do I need to play hostess or can you get your own?"

Joan smiled at her old aunty. "You sit still. We can serve ourselves, I'm sure." Cozy Mae nodded agreement, smiling. She disappeared into the igloo and came out with a mug of steaming tea with the bag tag draped over the side.

Joany followed suit but made her drink of choice coffee. She sunk her almost petite body onto a stump. "I like her, Aunty. I'm glad you called. With 15 children plus grands and 53,000 acres to put to work over the last 50 years, she has a literal horde of stories to share. And a tough row to hoe in the last few months." She sipped at her mug. "But you know all about all that.

I've invited her to spend a week with me for the 7-day 7-step fast track grief recovery program. We'll soon see what she decides."

Cozy Mae plunked into her oversize camp chair. "I'm so glad y'all made me get this, Sally. And I'm going to take Cousin Joan up on her offer. I know it won't get me over the haunting finer points that take time to assimilate, but I expect it will give me a running start toward the good stuff. At least there shouldn't be any more of the catty comebacks we experienced this morning. Those snide remarks are just not like me. I'll button it up and move to her place today."

Sally nodded approval. "Good for you, Coze. You won't be sorry for this decision. I know from experience."

Cozy tucked in wayward hair strands, "I understand she's just a mile or so away from here. It will be interesting to hear the difference in sounds of the screecher. I sure hope he gets nailed soon. It's positively frightening when he – or it – let's loose. Ruth Ann and Sparkle want to solve that mystery more than anything."

Sally chuckled. "As do we all. It's gone on way too long with no end in sight. I might task Rodney with zeroing in on where, precisely, it's coming from. That will give him a reason to not push me into making a rash decision about donkey happy hunting grounds."

Joan tilted her head and eyed Sally. "A rash decision about donkey happy hunting grounds? Are you considering locating donkey burial sites? That's wild even for you, old adventurous one."

Sally slapped her hand over her mouth, realizing she'd blabbed when she didn't want to. She wanted to work it out in her own mind first. Joany need never know if she decided against it. "Not quite, Joany. You missed out on the meeting of donkeys and mules yesterday. They were headed out for a better life up north. I'm thinking Rodney and I need to have a campout where the wild burros roam free."

Joany's eyes narrowed. She frowned. "A meeting of donkeys and mules... woman you're getting closer to me forcing you into a move you are fighting against. And it might first require a vacation in the looney bin." She splayed her hands toward Sally. "Explain, please."

Sally waved her aside. "Oh, my. Let me try to nutshell it for you…"

Joan nodded and sipped coffee… waiting and staring at Sally.

"Okay, Ms Officious. Here it is.

You remember the donkey that came home from Cozy Mae's with me?"

Joan nodded.

"Well, we finally learned his agenda. It took Sparkle and Ruth Ann to interpret; but they did a great job."

Joan swirled her hand to speed Sally up.

"Turns out, someone grabbed his parents but left him behind. I can't explain the how's of it all… He found them here. Along with a brother, a sister, and 2-half-brothers. They came to say goodbye. It's that simple." Sally recalled the picture she snapped. "Here they are."

Joan shook her head, grinning. "If you don't beat all, Aunty. And I have to go." She looked at Cozy Mae. "Are you ready to rumble over to my place?"

Cozy Mae stepped behind Sally and laid her hands on Sally's shoulders. "I'll wait until tomorrow. I need to be around here tonight."

Chapter 30 – The Simple Truth

"It wasn't necessary that you stay, Cozy." Sally said. "I'm all good."

"No, you're not. But mostly I felt like she was holding a gun to y'all's head. I don't know if I like her anymore."

"Achh," Sally waved it aside, "She just gets a little pushy now and again. She worries, as if me being over there on her place will prevent life from happening to me.

I like my place and my space. And I push back very well. But she's one that I want on my side every time. And she is. To the end."

Cozy Mae hunkered into her chair again. "I'm still staying here tonight unless you throw me out. Then I probably won't go. Deal with it."

Sally raised her hands up and smiled. "I give up, officer. And it is almost bedtime once again. Where are our children?" Sally peered around, listening for Ruth Ann's chatter. "Rodney! Where are you?" She shouted.

"Right here, milady." He came rolling around the igloo with Ruth Ann and Sparkle walking next to him. "We have a plan."

"Do you, now?" Sally gave him her full attention. "Do tell."

"Sparkle is sure he knows..."

"Wait, Rodney!" Ruth Ann cut in. "I am Sparkle's interpreter. I want to tell!"

"Then tell, Ruth Ann." Rodney said. "And thank you for not just blabbing over the top of my story. Sarcasm intended."

Ruth Ann's hair turned blue. "Here is the deal. Sparkle is positive that he knows the location of the screecher. But to catch him, we have to be at the place before he cuts loose.

We want to go there and hang out tonight. It is the same place we went to where we found the 3-toed footprint. We will be on a stakeout in private eye terms.

We can be there before dark if we start walking now." She gazed at Cozy Mae with her forehead creased. "Can we go, Em? Please, please, may we go solve this mystery?"

Cozy Mae did not hesitate. "No, ma'am! You may not walk across the desert at night! But," she eyed Sally, "we can all go in Sally's van and make a night of it. If Sally's up for it…"

Sally smiled, "Why not? But it's not going to happen until the wee hours of the morning. I say we take a nap and leave about midnight."

"Excuse me, milady."

"Yes, Rodney?"

"What if it is a movie set-up? They could all be there and gearing up before we arrive. I believe we should go now and find our stakeout spot early. We can take turns napping in the van so that someone is always monitoring the site."

"You have a point, Rodney. Okay. Let's button it up here and hit the road. We'll need cameras and night vision binoculars. And snacks. I'll grab a battery box in case one of you bots need a boost. And beverages. Cozy, will you grab those?"

Cozy Mae nodded. "We'll meet at y'all's van in 5-minutes. Come on kidlets."

By dark, the group was settled into the van at the observation post, practicing whispering.

Everybody was lined up on the bed with their backs against the wall and the long picture window their viewpoint. The windshield and back door windows were naked of curtains as well. Sparkle whined for a

THE SCREECHING SHADOWS OF HIDDEN VALLEY

curtain peek-around at the side of the van that was serving as backrests for Sally, Rodney, and Cozy Mae. Moving a tiny section of curtain aside for him, they could see a full 360°.

Sally felt her eyes getting heavy. "I'm closing my eyes for a bit. Wake me quietly in an hour or if anything happens before then."

The night drug on with no outside activity.

Sally plugged Rodney in for an hour... then moved the power supply cord to Ruth Ann; finishing with Sparkle.

She was proud of herself for grabbing the power bank with the teeny-tiny green LED that didn't light up the interior of the van. Even if the choice was an accident. It was really the battery box with the highest percentage of power available.

She and Cozy Mae ate their zip-top cans of soup with saltines. All three bots admonished "Shhhh..." when the cracker tube crinkled.

About 1 AM muffled voices sounded outside. Sally put the night vision binoculars up to her eyes. She recognized the little old lady dressed in an outrageous bejeweled caftan and a wizard's highly embellished cap with a bridal train trailing. She toddled onto the vacant lot from the direction of the rickety old adobe house they'd seen the other day.

"Rodney," she whispered. "Install the parabolic mic app again. And record what you hear."

"Yes, milady," he whispered back. "Recording now."

Sally was never able to sort out a word of what witch Hazel Bruja said. She hoped Rodney's parabolic app and recording device was working great.

Witch Hazel sat something on the ground and jabbered away to it. Sally focused her binoculars on the item. It was the tiniest of lizards – the one they call a dragon. A bearded dragon. Sally could see the tiny beard around its face. It was missing a left hind leg.

Hazel stepped back; pulled a wand from her pocket; swung the wand in the air like a conductor with his baton and began reciting. The recital went on and on. Finally, she ended it with a loud "G-G-Good!" that corresponded with a sharp snap of the wand.

Everybody but Rodney had to peel themselves from the ceiling when the tiny lizard with the missing hind leg exploded into a gigantic dragon right before their eyes. It screeched. It yowled. It roared. And spewed fire from its mouth. It hopped around on its one foot; never falling over.

Witch Hazel watched, reciting more incantations, and snapping her wand. A short time later the dragon shrunk to its normal teensy-weensy size, shaking its head like it had slurped a live bee into its mouth.

The witch picked the little lizard up again and toddled away, dragging her train behind her and muttering.

Chapter 31 – Mystery Solved

The self-proclaimed posse returned to Sally's compound. Not a word was spoken during the journey.

"I am going to bed. A'll see y'all later. Come children."

Sally got Rodney into his wheelchair and locked the van. They walked together to the vestibule of the igloo. Rodney kept going to his personal space. Only speaking to give Amy orders.

Sally, even though it was her usual wake up time, continued to her own bed. She changed into her nightie and tucked in.

Daylight came. Everyone slept, but Sally stirred. The daylight shined through her closed eyelids. She opened them and thought about what they'd witnessed.

She wondered if it was another far-out dream... but had no memory of bumping her head again. She got out of bed and padded to the kitchenette to start the coffee.

Cozy Mae knocked and came through the door, leaving it open for Ruth Ann and Sparkles. Sally poured the coffee and plunked onto her chair at the table. She traced the flowers that embellished the tablecloth.

"I guess I have to ask the question, Sally, before I check my own self into the so-called loony bin."

Sally froze and gazed at Cozy Mae. "Go ahead. Ask."

"Was it real? Did we see a little old lady dressed as a wizard conjure up a tiny lizard into a one-legged, fire spewing dragon?"

Sally wiped her forehead. "Phew! I was afraid to ask! But I have the same memory."

"Me, too, milady! I was afraid I had been invaded by viruses again. But I did not find any."

Ruth Ann butted in, "It was real. I knew it all the time. I was waiting for one of you to say it first because I did not want to be punished for making up stories that I knew as true."

Sparkle barked and whined. Ruth Ann smiled at him. "I know. You did not want to be put in a corner with a bag over your head, either."

"Did you get the recording, Rodney?" Sally asked.

"Oh! I was so worried about viruses that I forgot about that. Hang on. Let me look." Rodney bleeped and blipped. "Got it! Are you ready to hear it?"

Cozy Mae and Sally gaped at each other. Sally nodded. "Play it, Rodney!"

Here it comes:

'Thr-Thr-Thrice the brinded cat hath mew'd.
Thrice and once the hedge-pig whined.
Harpier cries 'Tis time, 'tis time.
Round about the cauldron go;
In the poison'd entrails throw.
T-T-Toad, that under cold stone
Days and nights has thirty-one
Swelter'd venom sleeping got,
Boil thou first i' the charmed pot.
Double, double toil and trouble;
Fire burn, and cauldron bubble.
F-F-F-Fillet of a fenny snake,
In the cauldron boil and bake;
Eye of newt and toe of frog,
Wool of bat and tongue of dog,

THE SCREECHING SHADOWS OF HIDDEN VALLEY

*Adder's fork and blind-worm's sting,
L-L-L-Lizard's leg and owlet's wing,
For a charm of powerful trouble,
Like a hell-broth boil and bubble.
Double, double toil and trouble;
Fire burn and cauldron bubble.
Scale of dragon, tooth of wolf,
Witches' mummy, maw and gulf
Of the ravin'd salt-sea shark,
R-R-Root of hemlock digg'd i' the dark,
Liver of blaspheming Jew,
Gall of goat, and slips of yew
Sliver'd in the moon's eclipse,
Nose of Turk and Tartar's lips,
Finger of birth-strangled babe
Ditch-deliver'd by a drab,
Make the gruel thick and slab:
Add thereto a tiger's chaudron,
For the ingredients of our cauldron.
Double, double toil and trouble;
Fire burn and cauldron bubble.
Cool it with a baboon's blood,
Then the charm is firm;
Your leg is back and you are G-G-Good!'*

"That's it, milady. But that incantation sounds very much like Macbeth's three witches spell scene, with stammers. And it didn't work now, either."

Sally laughed. "If I had any question of who that was, I don't anymore. Rodney, do you remember witch Hazel Bruja? The stammering old woman who claimed to be 193 years old when

Spaghettio came... We all feared one of her spells got away from her and turned a kitty into a crazed attack cat.

"Oh, milady. How could I forget? That's how my foot got mangled."

"But what do we do about it?" Sally asked. "Nobody will believe it. Not even Mulriley.

Is she hurting anybody now that the chaparral has already been turned to char? There shouldn't be any more fires to put out in a hurry. Is she hurting the lizard?"

"Well, milady. According to everythingreptilion.com, the lizard is able to grow back its own leg. Perhaps we should keep it our little secret; let nature take its course; and enthrall a little old lady's heart. That might be what keeps her going... But I might have to tell Teague..."

Sally nodded. "Good thought, Rodney. I'm for it. But not for sharing with Teague. That could come back to bite you."

Cozy Mae nodded. "I agree. I'm leaving, Sally. It's you and Rodney who will have to listen to the screeching roars. But, at least, y'all will know that witch Hazel is trying again."

"Wait!" Ruth Ann broke in. "Does this mean I cannot tell anyone this story? But it is true!"

"Ruth Ann," Cozy Mae explained, "It's our little secret because no one will believe it. Y'all could find yourself in a corner with a bag over your head for making up wild stories."

"*Our greatest weakness lies in giving up. The most certain way to succeed is always to try just one more time.*" — Thomas A. Edison

ALEXIE LINN

I HOPE YOU ENJOYED *The Screeching Shadows of Hidden Valley*. **Find your next fun and interesting book and audiobook at** https://alexielinnauthor.com

And tell others how fun and interesting this read was at Goodreads[1], Bookbub[2], or your other favorite review place. But tell *me here* about any egadses that got past the editing and review team. Thank you.

---

1. https://www.goodreads.com/search?q=alexie+linn&qid=wKbuakNcqZ
2. https://www.bookbub.com/search?search=alexie%20linn

THE SCREECHING SHADOWS OF HIDDEN VALLEY

Step into a world of mystery, adventure, and heartwarming resilience in Alexie Linn's captivating stories.

From a young girl sharing tales with her feline companions to a woman finding solace in writing after loss, these interconnected stories will keep you on the edge of your seat.

Meet Joan Freed, the rebel life coach navigating life twists's and turns, and follow Mary Linn, her spirited niece, as she unravels family secrets in graveyards. Join Sally the Loner on her unpredictable journey filled with ghostly surprises and unexpected luck.

Alexie's stories will take you on a rollercoaster of emotions, from laughter to tears, as you explore the complexities of life and love. Explore the desert southwest with this talented storyteller and let her captivating narratives transport you to a world of wonder and discovery.

Alexie Linn writes from experience and a vivid imagination. She writes from her desert southwest off-grid home in Arizona.

Don't miss out!

Visit the website below and you can sign up to receive emails whenever Alexie Linn publishes a new book. There's no charge and no obligation.

https://books2read.com/r/B-A-YYUD-KFTIF

BOOKS 2 READ

Connecting independent readers to independent writers.

Did you love *The Screeching Shadows of Hidden Valley*? Then you should read *Secrets of the Tainted Trough*[3] by Alexie Linn!

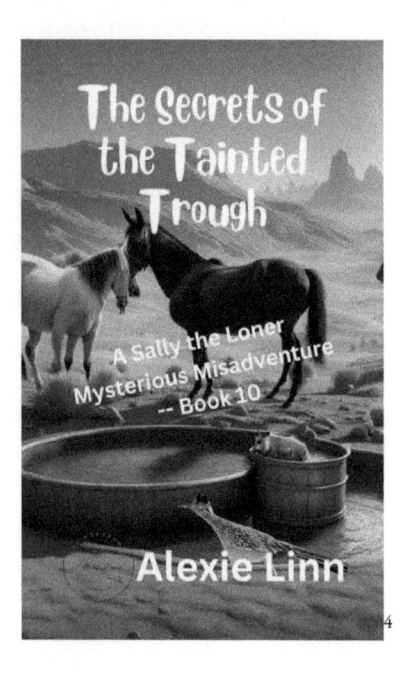

In "The Secrets of the Tainted Trough", imagine waking up from a nap to see a donkey and a horse peering through the screen door, both desperately thirsty. Would you give them a drink? And then what?

Sally, an energetic 87-year-old woman, faces this exact dilemma. Intrigued by the animals, she decides to investigate why they keep returning to her property. What she discovers shocks her to the core - their water trough is contaminated with a body. But whose body is it? And how did it end up in the water trough?

With no one else around but a goat, chickens and a pup, Sally wonders if the body could be their missing caregiver. As the mystery

---

3. https://books2read.com/u/boXOZa

4. https://books2read.com/u/boXOZa

deepens, she must grapple with the fate of both the animals and the unknown person in the trough.

Join Sally on her thrilling and perplexing journey as she unravels the truth behind this mysterious misadventure.

Prepare to be captivated by the twists and turns in "The Secrets of the Tainted Trough", a tale filled with suspense, intrigue, and unexpected revelations.

Read more at https://alexielinnauthor.com.

Also by Alexie Linn

A Life Changing Joan Freed Mystery Adventure
The Personal Transformation of Queenie
Elaine The Hoarder
Rescue Me!
The Mount Saint Helens Affair
The Aurora Borealis Affair
The Vintage Trailer
Blindsided!
Ruby, the Haunted
Azalia's Bizarre Dilemma

Genealogy and Family History
Your Fascinating Family History – In 7 Eye-Opening Steps

Mary Linn, Gravestone Hunter
Mary Linn, Gravestone Hunter
Bodies Lost and Found
Mary Linn, Gravestone Hunter Book 2
The Empty Grave, Book 3

Sally the Loner
Sally the Loner Meets the Sourdough Kid
The Auctionhouse Murders
Sally Wins the Lottery -- But She Didn't Buy the Ticket
The Mysterious Mistresses of Mormon Lake Lodge
Sally and Alliwicious...
The Sourdough Bakeoff
The Truth About Bobby
The Git-Buggy Murders?
Sally vs the Marauders: The Case for the Defense
Secrets of the Tainted Trough
The Tangled Tails of Spaghettio: A Whisker Raising Mystery
The Goat that Wasn't; A Baa-d Mystery
The Procrastinator's Perpetual Planning Calendar
Planet Ziggy Expedition: The Phoenix Lights Mystery
Bones of Contention
Too Many Bodies and a Burro
The Screeching Shadows of Hidden Valley

Scarecrow
I Am Scarecrow
Scarecrow Sells the Farm
Scarecriow Finds His Shadow
Scarecrow Gets Three Wishes
A Bundle of Scarecrows

Your Plucky New Life -- On Purpose
True Secret Shopper Diaries -- How NOT To Get Caught

The Skinny On Sourdough

Standalone
Adventures in Retort Canning

Watch for more at https://alexielinnauthor.com.

About the Author

Alexie's characters will take you on a rollercoaster of emotions, from laughter to tears, as you explore the complexities of life and love. Explore the desert southwest with this talented storyteller and let her captivating narratives transport you to a world of wonder and discovery.

Alexie Linn writes from experience and a vivid imagination. She writes from her desert southwest off-grid home in Arizona.

Read more at https://alexielinnauthor.com.